MURDER
IN
PALM BEACH

MURDER
IN
PALM BEACH

●

Cat Lyons

AVALON BOOKS
NEW YORK

PRINTED IN THE UNITED STATES OF AMERICA
ON ACID-FREE PAPER
BY HADDON CRAFTSMEN, BLOOMSBURG, PENNSYLVANIA

For my father, with love and gratitude

Chapter One

Low, peering over the back of the boat, a head appeared. Dripping wet, eyes bright, gasping, sodden, it—she—was nonetheless exquisite. A perfectly dreamlike face: ski jump nose, rosy cheeks, petulant chin and big hesitant eyes, framed with slick wisps and curls of short sandy blonde hair.

Dan stared. What with the sunset, the stars, and Phoebe Snow warbling easy in his ears, it wasn't such a terrible way to spend a lonely evening, just floating off into a lazy little dream. The vision of a pretty girl was a nice addition. He was mostly content to just gaze upon the angelic face, never thinking it could be real, not really thinking much at all.

She got prettier as she came closer. A slender white neck rose like a stem. Thin hands grappled the stainless steel rail, long arms glowed in the starlight. Her T-shirt was sop-

1

ping wet. Dan's interest piqued but he didn't stir, not wanting to risk derailing the muse. He grinned softly, and remained stretched out long and flat on the cushion down in the shadows of the deck. It wasn't until droplets of water splattered his bare leg that he truly began to wonder: *was the mirage real?* He sat up.

Teri was on the deck when she saw the darkness move. Falling down onto her haunches, she was ready to leap overboard and hide in the water.

"Hey," muttered Dan. Yanking off the headphones, he repeated, "Hey," this time a bit more loudly, but then his attention was led away from the mirage and across the bay. Sirens blared in the night and lights from the anchored boats blazed. Phoebe, the big stars, and the mirage had taken him far away, and he was having difficulty navigating back. His tongue was loose and ready to speak but his mind sputtered. Finally Dan managed, "Uh, you . . . okay?"

Teri wasn't eager to get back in the water. She hadn't figured out much, but that she knew. "Me . . . okay." She mocked him. Like Dan, she was also suffering from a mind short-circuiting experience.

Dan allowed a grin. He didn't mind being mocked; a sense of humor was good. "They looking for you?"

"Could be." She ducked before a search beam bathed Dan and the deck in blinding light.

Dan froze. He squinted. He lifted a hand to shield his eyes. It was slow going but things were beginning to add up.

An outboard roared. With siren baying, a black inflatable raft approached; the rubber side bounced against Dan's boat. Two men in boots, helmets and life jackets—or were they bullet proof vests?—vaulted out onto the deck. Each had a hand on a gun. Two more men stayed in the powerboat, one at the engine controls, one on the bow with a spotlight. With a shove and a rumble the boat edged away and began to circle the sailboat, the spotlight scanning down along the hull and out across the black water.

"What's going on?" Dan mumbled. He forced himself not to look around.

"Police," someone barked. "Sorry to disturb you." The cop closest to him flashed open something that Dan never saw but took to be an ID. Already the cop was opening lockers, nosing inside, mumbling, "We are in pursuit of a criminal suspect." The other cop took a quick turn about the foredeck, his flashlight peering over the edge, probing into the anchor locker and each sail bag. Then he vaulted down into the cabin. The first cop dropped the hatch lid and it banged hard. "Have you seen anyone tonight?"

Dan murmured thoughtfully, "Have I seen—"

"Someone swimming."

"Swimming? No. I didn't see anyone swimming."

"Mind if we look around?"

Dan thought about that, too. He said, "I guess."

The cop nodded and ducked below. Cupboards, closets and lockers were thrown open. Every cabin light was on. Bags were yanked out.

"Hey." Dan leaned in. "My stuff."

The nearest cop, the one in the galley, added a doleful glance as he suggested, "Sir, could you wait out on the deck."

"But . . ."

The police boat was back alongside. The cop at the helm

flicked on his flashlight and shone it into Dan's face. "Why didn't your boat have any lights on?"

Dan shrugged. "I was just . . . you know, star gazing." The truth was, if he wasn't actually looking at anything, he preferred the dark, relaxing under starlight, contemplating the mysteries of life.

The policeman's eyes narrowed. He glanced up swiftly as if to check on these alleged stars, then back at Dan. "Sir, it's against the law not to use an anchor light." He barked when he spoke, they all barked whenever they spoke. "I could cite you right now, and confiscate your boat. It's a navigation hazard and a serious offense."

Dan craned his neck, pretending to check the fixture at the top of the mast. It was a clear and moonless night, a beautiful night. Despite the glare of terrestrial lights the stars were bright and clear. Dan reached in the companion-way, and flicked a switch. He grimaced. "Darn bulb must've blown."

"You carry a spare?"

Slowly Dan nodded like he was pondering a novel idea. He agreed, "I should."

Down below the cop finished checking the oven and he took the lid off the icebox.

Dan watched his boat being ransacked.

"Sir, you better fix that light right away."

Dan half nodded. He muttered, "Yeah, I will." He wondered if the cop meant now, right now, right this instant. He didn't feel much like fixing it right now. Dan sidled over towards the lifelines, towards the helmsman cop. It amazed him how all the cops looked the same, the way they bounded around barking at each other. Dan spent a moment considering that before he shook the thought out of his head and asked what he wanted to ask. "So, who is it you're looking for?" He almost yelled to be heard over the rumble of the big twin outboards.

The cop carefully scrutinized Dan's approach. "Not at liberty to say, sir."

Dan shrugged. "Should I be worried? I mean, after you go, if I see someone, are they dangerous? I'm alone; I don't have a gun or anything. What did they do?" As he said it he realized he had almost said what did *she* do.

The cop announced, "The individual is a murder suspect."

"Wow," Dan mouthed.

"You should be careful, sir."

"Yeah. Yeah, I will."

The two policemen thumped up the companionway. They leapt over the lifelines and onto the powerboat. One of them said, "Thank you for your cooperation, sir."

Dan nodded. The boat roared off, skimming across the flat calm water to another sailboat nearby. Standing on deck he continued to watch the cops board and begin another search, same routine. *How could all the cops look and act the same?* He flicked a switch and the light in the fore peak went off.

Dan's mind drifted to the wet nymph, and he wondered about her. A moment later, from the master panel he switched off all the lights.

"Hey," she whispered close behind.

He turned. "Hey."

The big search beam spun over Dan's boat and circled past.

"Let's get below."

He needn't have said anything. She was already down the companionway hunkered low, shivering. "Why'd you do that?"

"What?"

"Lie to the police."

Good question. He gave it careful consideration. He watched the water as he filled the kettle. He looked at her, and could discover only one plausible explanation: she was beautiful. "You don't know why?" Dan turned off the spigot.

Teri shook her head. "You'll be in big trouble if they catch me here."

She was right—he *would* be in big trouble. "Well, it just didn't seem fair, all those cops with their guns and flashy equipment—and one soggy little girl. It's like the fox and the hounds . . . who doesn't root for the fox?"

"I see." Absently, she began tidying up the mess the police left, putting cans of beans back in a bin, putting mugs back in the cupboard.

He squeezed by Teri in the narrow cabin, found a towel and handed it to her. *Did he just feel sorry for the poor outnumbered fox?* he wondered. "So, why are they after you?" He glanced at her.

Teri rubbed her head with the towel. She wore tan shorts and a white T-shirt emblazoned with *Felix the Cat*. He found he was developing a strong new appreciation for *Felix the Cat* and forced himself to look away.

"I mean, one look at you and I figured, you know, you aren't the type to have committed some serious crime, are you? It's some sort of mistake."

"Yes." She shivered, wiping down her legs with the towel, rubbing her feet.

"Good." Dan said with enthusiasm. "I'm glad to hear that. They're after the wrong girl."

"No."

"No?"

"Not really. It's me they want."

"Oh," Dan lost a little enthusiasm. "You *are* the murderer?"

"Seems like." Teri felt only a numb awareness. Yes, they were after her, she knew that, but it didn't seem possible. She didn't believe it. Nothing seemed real. Every so often she had to zip away and watch the dilemma from a comfortable height, then she was yanked back and dropped into the middle of chaos and everything was real again, everything . . . but that wasn't possible, so off she'd zip again. Zipping up and down like a yo-yo.

Dan thought about murder and all that the word 'murderer' implied. He opened the lid on the ice box, stuck his head down. "Hungry?"

"A little."

His head reappeared. He held something thin in a ziplock bag. "So, anyway, where were you hiding?"

"Up the mast."

"Really?"

"Very top."

"Cool." Dan dropped the plastic bag outside on the deck. "You just shimmied up?"

"Yeah. Kept moving around trying to hide behind it. Trying not to fall."

"Don't think I could shimmy up that mast." He squeezed by her. The aisle was narrow in the boat.

"I didn't think I could either, but I didn't have much choice."

He sorted through clothes, stuffing some away in a bin behind the settee. Then he stopped and handed her sweat pants and a T-shirt. "They won't fit, but I think they're pretty clean. They're dry anyhow."

"Thanks." Teri went forward. They brushed by each other again. She shut the door to the cramped little compartment and locked it.

Dan put coffee beans in the grinder. As he gave it a blast he glimpsed out the port. Now there was a helicopter flailing away overhead, a cone of blinding light pouring down from its belly. Stepping up into the companionway he noticed another search boat working its way along the far shore. There were cop cars spread around the neighborhood, among the big houses. Lights were on everywhere. He crossed the cockpit to the stern rail and flipped open the lid of the barbecue, turned on the gas, and lit it.

Teri stood at the base of the companionway ladder, looking waif-like in the oversized clothes. The Maple Leaf T-shirt reached her knees and the sweats were rolled up like donuts around her calves. She looked lost and tiny—bedraggled, but prettier than ever.

He gazed at her. *What is he now, an accessory after aiding and abetting? Something like that. But she's a murderer?* Dan was having trouble digesting some of these concepts. "Murder, right?"

"Yes."

Someone important?" He looked away and began to unwrap the plastic bag. "Must've been. This is a pretty big fuss."

"Thomas Jefferson Hill."

He glanced back and shook his head. "Who's that?"

"Who's that! Where are you from?"

"Canada mostly." A sizzle flared as Dan dropped two steaks on the grill. He turned to her and called, "Boyfriend?"

"No."

"Self-defense or something?"

"No, not really."

"Not really? Kind of self-defense?"

"No."

"Ah, that's too bad. Self-defense would've been good: get a good lawyer, tell the police, big fuss but everything would maybe be okay in the end."

"Not this time."

He stared at the steaks thinking—*not this time, not this time*—then added, "Just one murder, right?"

"Just one."

"I mean career-wise."

"It's not a career."

"Well, that's good." He reached down and grabbed the plastic squirt bottle of barbecue sauce as the kettle struggled to whistle. "Can you get that?"

Teri poured water into the coffee press. Dan flipped the steaks. "Medium?"

"Medium rare."

He told her about the French bread and the antipasto and she prepped them and set out plates and cutlery.

"Let's eat on the desk, enjoy the view."

It didn't seem like a good idea to her. Nonetheless she came up carrying a plate in each hand, and it was somehow comforting to once more be out in the open and under the stars.

Dan leaned over and dumped one steak on each plate. "Hope it's done the way you like."

The anchorage was still awash in flashing lights and wailing sirens, but it was a nice night: cool, calm, clear. They stretched out on either side of the deck, backs against the coach roof, knees pulled up, feet flat.

Teri took the steak knife and sliced off a piece. "Looks perfect." She forked it into her mouth.

"So, what was it? Gun? Candle stick? Lead pipe?"

"Knife. Hey, this is really good."

"Thanks. A knife, wow! Killed a guy with a knife."

She sliced off another chunk. "I'm Teri, by the way."

"Dan." He offered his hand. She thought his hand was nice and warm. He liked the cool smooth softness of hers.

"The meal is really terrific. Thanks, I didn't realize how hungry I was."

"I bet you've had a busy day."

Teri shrugged. *A busy day? You could say that.* She felt numb. She was content to feel numb. She didn't want to think.

Meditatively he munched on a hunk of baguette.

"Listen, Teri, I'm still not clear on this self-defense thing. You said it wasn't really self-defense, but that makes me think it might've been just a little teeny bit self-defense. There may be an opportunity there."

Teri shook her head. She was beginning to tire. The shivers had stopped. She felt cozy in the baggy clothes, but every time she relaxed and freed her mind to wander, she started to shiver and panic and see things that just couldn't be.

"Well," Dan said, "what do I know? I'm not a lawyer or anything. Maybe you should talk to a lawyer."

This guy was pretty weird—seemed so blasé about the manhunt and a murderess climbing aboard his boat. She hadn't figured out if she wanted to discuss her predicament with him, so she didn't speak, just shrugged and said, "Maybe."

They finished dinner. Dan slipped below and back. Then they nibbled on chocolate chip cookies and sipped coffee as the big noisy helicopter hovered overhead. The light bore down on their little boat. They were concealed beneath the dodger, but Dan leaned out and stood. He stared up at the bright light, then said, "Gee, that's a heck of a bright light."

The helicopter left. It took a while but eventually a lone police boat remained to cruise around, mostly by the shoreline. Several police cars were still parked among the houses at the head of the bay. Sirens sang out occasionally. It was becoming more like a normal night in Lake Worth.

"Looks like they're beginning to give up."

Teri finished a swig and swallowed. "Yeah, I guess I should get going."

"Going? Yeah right," he scoffed, then stopped, "Really? Going? What, swim away?"

"Can I keep the T-shirt and sweats?"

"No." There was no clue he was joking. In fact his face gave no indication he even knew what a sense of humor was, always gaunt and dark, even when he laughed.

Teri hadn't made a move to leave. They sat a while

longer in the darkness, watching the activity dwindle and the stars grow bigger still.

"You should get your anchor light fixed."

"It works fine. I just didn't want to turn it on right then." His coffee long gone, he put down the mug. "Look, you might as well spend the night."

Teri said, "I should go. I've imposed enough, I mean . . ."

"It's okay, no big deal."

"Listen Dan, I can't thank you enough. You've been great but . . . I'll send a card, or something."

"A card'd be nice."

"Yeah right."

"Seriously. Heck, you're a murderer right? You think I'm crazy?"

She wasn't going to answer that. *Was this guy for real?* He didn't show any signs of being afraid of her or anything. Tough, rugged, tall and sinewy, he looked like someone that you wouldn't want to meet in a dark alley. *He* was afraid of *her*? If he was handsome it was in some sinister or scary way. It was hard to tell in the dark, but his eyes seemed to hide some distant gentleness. And his calm voice was comforting. Actually, she realized, she had no choice *but* to trust him. "I saw only one bunk down there. I'll sleep out here in the cockpit."

"Yeah right," his voice slightly mimicked hers. "Out here with the cops and the rain?" It didn't look the least bit like rain. "You take the bunk."

"I couldn't. Where will you sleep?"

"Here." He indicated the cockpit with a shrug.

"In the rain?"

"It's not going to rain. Heavy dew, maybe." Dan looked around. He gathered up the dishes and returned down the companionway steps. He kept looking around like he'd never seen his boat before. The quarter berth was big, the only real bed on the boat, every inch a double. The settees were narrow and were not padded.

Teri sat on the edge of the quarter berth. The mattress was just right, soft yet firm. It would be cozy, and she was tired.

"I can sleep on the cabin sole," he announced stoically. Dan spread his hands out to indicate what a splendid bed the hardwood cabin floor would make.

He waited, head still down, nodding slowly.

Teri waited. She stopped plumping up the pillow.

Dan stood but didn't move, certainly made no attempt at preparing to sleep on the floor.

"Look this bunk is big enough for two, as long as . . ."

Critically, Dan assessed the roominess of the quarter berth. "Okay." He nodded slowly. "I'll try my best."

Teri snickered, then said sternly, "Back to back. Nose against the wall." She laughed again; it was a fragile laugh that grated in her throat. She moved outboard as far as she could.

Dan slid shut the companionway hatch, locking it. He went to the head then came back and slipped in beside her. Reaching up he flicked off the last light. Scrunching into his pillow he pulled up the blanket.

It was almost dark. Silvery starlight slipped in the ports, and the electrical panel emitted pinpoints of faint red glow. All was quiet.

Teri shuddered as a vivid memory accosted her. She felt a quiver and tears began to well.

In a deeply contemplative voice, Dan said. "This person—the person you killed, it wasn't while they slept was it?"

"No."

"I mean, I just did you a favor and all. I could have told the cops I'd seen you." He was half-kidding, half cajoling her to talk. "I, uh, stuck my neck out for you and all."

"Thanks, I really—"

"And the meal was okay?"

"Great."

"So . . ."

"Don't worry, I won't kill you while you sleep."

"Promise?"

"Yes, I promise."

He reached back and found her hands. He checked if her fingers were crossed. *Gosh they were nice soft hands—too nice to hold a knife.* "Okay then, it's a promise. Goodnight."

"Goodnight." She snuggled a little into her pillow.

"And really, thanks."

Their bodies touched lightly. Teri didn't pull away. She found the warmth of his body, distant as it was, comforting. "This is the weirdest day of my life."

Dan nodded. He could understand that.

A few minutes later she spoke again. She felt like crying. Her eyes wouldn't close. Every time they did, she saw things. "Dan?"

He murmured, "Yeah."

"I lied about killing someone. I didn't."

"That's great." His voice was soft. "I had this hunch you didn't. You don't seem the type." He spoke so gently the words seemed to reach out and touch her. They slipped along her spine soothing her jangled nerves. It was just another thing that didn't seem possible; the guy looked like a pirate, and acted like a buffoon. He scared her, kept her off balance yet somehow comforted her at the same time. Nothing seemed to shock him.

She gave up thinking. She spoke, just spoke freely as if in a trance, no longer thinking first. "I could never kill anyone, you know, not for any reason." She shrugged and said it again, "At least, I don't *think* I could. But everyone is so sure I did. So I guess I was feeling angry or sorry for myself. So I just said I did—to get it over with."

"Sometimes, I don't think I think much like anyone else."

That was certainly the impression she was getting. "I'm glad."

There was a long pause. "Teri?" Another pause and then he said, "You okay?"

"Yes. No. I don't know." She whispered, "I'm really tired."

"Okay, we'll talk again in the morning. Try not to worry."

Teri didn't answer. She pretended to be asleep and wondered what to do. The guy was a flake, but a nice flake. He acted as if he knew her, or at least cared about her, as though nothing particularly shocking had happened. And amazingly she had found herself falling in line and acting the same. It seemed a better idea than panicking. So half of Palm Beach County was searching for her, big deal; so they thought she'd murdered the one and only T J Hill; so every time she closed her eyes she saw blood, felt herself covered in hot blood, heard cries and screams—everything would turn out okay . . . somehow.

Maybe she could talk to this Dan guy; it'd be nice to have someone. Maybe she could trust him. *Who else was there?*

Maybe.

Or maybe not. When she woke up in the morning he was gone.

Chapter Two

Maybe he woke up, realized what a fool he'd been, and went for the police. Teri stared at the dent in his pillow. She shouldn't be surprised—that's exactly what she would have done. Still, she was surprised. She didn't want to think he'd gone for the cops, but the thought had to be considered because—she heard her own high pitched wail reverberate inside her head—*where else could he be?*

Reality lodged in her throat. Somehow with Dan her predicament had seemed sort of surreal. Now she couldn't breathe. She wanted to get away, fast and far. She craved action: to get back in the water, but swim where? Swim until exhaustion dragged her down to oblivion? That was an option that Teri considered. She glimpsed out the port. Someone would see her swimming—the sun was starting to rise. Someone would be having breakfast in one of those tall white condos, in a solarium, look up and notice a woman swimming in Lake Worth. The cops would swoop down like eagles and scoop her up. She'd be caught and caged, taunted and poked at like a homicidal lunatic freak. *Nobody would listen. Why would anyone listen?*

Maybe she could steal the sailboat and make a run for the Atlantic; sail off into the big blue ocean. Maybe that's what Dan wanted her to do. Maybe that's why he left her alone. She didn't know much about boats, but maybe she could figure it out. No—impossible.

It was cozy in the bunk. The air was cool and fresh with just a slight salty tang. Maybe she should just wait right here for the police. Her muscles tingled from last night's hectic exertions. *What to do?* Teri moaned, stretched, closed her eyes and as she struggled to catch her breath, there it was again.

Hot blood.

Like watching herself in a movie.

> Hill convulsing, staring up, eyes huge. She's kneeling beside him, her hand beneath his head. He can't breathe. Blood trickles from the corners of his mouth. The hilt of the knife is in her fist. She pulls it from his chest. Trying to help, she pulls it from the base of Hill's throat. Now the blood is chugging in erratic spurts. Her hand is on the wound trying to staunch the flow. And it stops. Stops completely, even when she removes her hand. Every part of Mr. Hill stops moving. He's dead. She's too shocked to scream or cry. His eyes keep staring.

Teri battled the memory, trying to understand but not remember. She whimpered. Tears welled up. She couldn't escape the vacant gaze of the dead man. The eyes remained before her, until:

"What? What have you done?" It's Zabbits. Behind her.

"No." She gasps.

"You, you stabbed him!"

"No, no, I . . ."

Zabbits has a gun. He's pointing it at her.

She's just standing, sticky with blood, holding the knife.

"No."

She staggers towards Zabbits, her own eyes wide with terror. He too, looks like he's in shock. He's afraid of her, afraid of the knife. He raises his gun. He fires. Teri tries to scream, but can't. The gun kicks high, and before Zabbits can aim he fires again and again and the gun jolts up wilder and wider, shattering first the big window, then thumping into the ceiling. Somehow she's down on the lawn running.

She's dropped the knife.

At the edge of the water Teri stops. Everywhere there is noise, and people calling 'Stop her, stop her.' Then the sirens start far away.

Teri remembered thinking *Sirens, police, I'm saved.*

Another gunshot. The sirens are getting closer. Another gunshot: and it's very close, she hears the bullet sizzle through the night air. People are coming. Another shot. She doesn't know what to do. *What to do?* People are shooting at her!

Teri had started to sob and tremble, straining to get a hold of herself when a bump on the stern startled her back to reality. *Someone was here.* She wanted to get up and flee but she couldn't stop shaking.

Something about the quiet, easy way he climbed aboard—it must be Dan. She knew before he came and bent under the dodger. Teri started breathing again. Squeezing her eyes closed she crawled out of the bunk.

Black stubble stood like coarse sandpaper on his chin, cheeks and down his long gaunt throat. He was undeniably handsome, but in a sinister, frightening fashion. She'd always dated pretty boys with peach fuzz, pink complexions and wavy blonde hair, and not too tall. Dan was towering tall, and his hair was short, black and spiky. No one would mistake him for pretty. You don't fool with a man like this, that's what his appearance said. But his actions were all kind and gentle, his eyes warm pools of easy blue light.

"Hey," he said as he handed her the front section of the paper.

It was this morning's paper she could tell by the pictures. Yesterday's didn't have pictures of her on the front page. "Great," she moaned.

"Could be worse. You look good, nice picture." Dan picked up two bags of groceries and a gallon of fresh squeezed orange juice.

"What does it say?" she asked. Stories about the murder covered the front page.

"The guy was a genuine saint and you killed him. If I didn't know you so well, I'd be convinced you were the murderer."

"Just great."

He placed the groceries on the counter and flicked on the VHF radio. "Lot of compelling evidence."

"I bet there is."

In the galley Dan began to open the bags. "Don't know what you like for breakfast, so I got," he announced each item as he hauled it out, "eggs, bacon, ham, sausage, croissants, cinnamon rolls. Also bagels, cream cheese, yogurt . . . and let's see, two types of melon, strawberries, kiwi, green grapes, red grapes, bananas and these great navel oranges." He looked into the bag but there was nothing else there. Then he said, "So, what would you like?"

Teri peeked out from behind the paper. The bounty overflowed the small counter. She hesitated.

"I can make pancakes," Dan added. "Take about ten minutes."

"Oh dear."

"French toast? I make good French toast. Canadian maple syrup and everything."

"You're going to kill me."

"Let's not start the day off with any more of that." He turned, struck a match and lit the stove.

She loved French toast, but she didn't want him to go to so much trouble. "Well, I saw some Fruit Loops last night and I have a real craving."

"No problem at all." He smiled, and with his long left arm he pushed the groceries aside. "Fruit Loops all around." He got the box, two bowls and the milk.

They sat sideways at the settee table, feet up on the bench seats. Teri poured cereal as she read the front page. Dan added the milk and they started to munch, heads down. He pulled out the sports section. They had coffee and broke into the cinnamon buns.

Teri finished all the articles she could handle and pushed the paper away. "I'm doomed."

"Sure looks like it." Dan didn't look up from his section. "So are the Leafs. Not even going to make the playoffs this year."

"I might as well give up and turn myself in."

"You could." Dan licked his sticky fingers and turned the page. Two minutes later he turned another page. "Have they got capital punishment in this state?"

"Yes, I think so."

Dan nodded, then grimaced. "Ouch." He kept reading the paper. The last few pages were all ads so he folded it up and stared at her.

Without enthusiasm Teri suggested, "Maybe I could cut a deal?"

"Maybe." He nodded.

Impatient, she squirmed a little.

Dan asked, "You mean like confess?"

Teri stopped and thought about that.

Dan poured more coffee. "I think that's what cutting a deal amounts to: confessing." He took a sip, swallowed, looked first at his cup then directly into her eyes. "Thinking of confessing to a murder you didn't do?"

Teri looked away. "Maybe then I wouldn't get the chair, or whatever it is they use."

"That's true." He picked up another section of the paper. "Probably just get life in jail. That's pretty good."

Nothing was real—Dan, the boat, the breakfast, the newspaper—especially the newspaper. The pictures of her, stories about her, lies about her, none of it felt real. Anxiety was creeping up her spine, she felt she might suddenly shudder to bits. Teri looked at Dan. He had flipped to the comics. It infuriated her. *How could he be so calm? Easy,* she answered herself, *he isn't being charged with murder.* But still—he was grinning at *Peanuts*, at *Peanuts* for crying out loud, like it was just a lazy Sunday morning and nothing was wrong. But something was terribly wrong. It wasn't Sunday and *Peanuts* was sometimes cute, but never really funny, and the world thought she had killed Thomas Jefferson Hill. Terror was welling up inside her. She was having trouble breathing. She shook her head. *What can I do?* Her voice rose, "What can I do?"

Dan put the paper down. "About the murder thing?"

"Of course," she gasped, then her voice cracked shrilly, "about the murder thing!"

"Yeah. You know," he said, "I've been thinking about that a lot." He took his time. It was like he knew a hurricane was swirling around him, but he strove to remain in the center, in the calm, even if it was only the eye. She could see him thinking, like he was working on an idea. "But I don't know what to do. I wish I did. I'm sorry."

For an instant she had dreamed he might magically say something that would save her, at least give her hope. "Well, I can't just stay here."

"Oh." He folded over his paper. "Why not?"

"Because!"

Dan took a swig of coffee and reached for another sticky bun. "Sorry you feel that way. But for now I think maybe you should." He pushed the buns over to her.

"What? Just stay here on your boat?" She shoved the buns away.

"It's a little cramped I guess, but better than treading water. At least you can relax a bit and think."

"Relax!"

"Yeah." He took a bite, chewed, swallowed, and reached for his coffee. "I know, I know it's almost impossible, I understand that, but I think you have to try." He took another bite.

She snorted her contempt, then began to toy with the package. Finally she took one, but didn't eat it, just tapped the bun on her plate. "I can't just stay here."

"No? Have you got somewhere else in mind?"

Teri paused, then shook her head.

"Well . . ." Dan shrugged.

"Is that okay with you? Me staying here?"

"Sure, it's great."

"Great?" Teri asked, "Why great?"

"I mean, it's okay." Dan shrugged again. "It's fine. No problem. I don't mind." He picked up another section of the paper and began to read.

Teri scowled. She stared ahead blankly. Finally she took another sip of coffee. It was really good coffee, went well with the sticky buns, like the one she still jostled in her hand. She couldn't believe she was thinking of eating another one, but what difference did fat and calories make now? Picking up the paper she tried to read *Peanuts*. Ultimately she worked her way through all the comics and the coffee and the bun, and dropped the newspaper back onto the table.

"Dan, I don't want to drag you into this."

"It's okay."

He was trying so hard. For an instant the tension vanished. She found herself almost smiling.

Their eyes met and he grinned like he was reading her thoughts. "I . . . like having you around."

Did he do this outrageous stuff just to shock her? Was it a way of distracting her from her ordeal? She looked away to the package of buns and finally gave it a shove then looked back and waited for their eyes to meet again. The smile faded. Softly she pleaded, "Dan, I don't know what to do."

He was caught in her eyes, and a hint of warmth crept up into his mouth. Content to speak slowly, he said, "Really want me to advise you on what to do?"

"Maybe."

"Remember, I'm nobody." He picked up his coffee mug and watched it dangle from a long index finger. "I don't know nothing, but . . ."

She waited, thinking to herself *That's a double negative* and she hated double negatives but she wasn't about to tell him that, then she saw a glint in his eyes like he understood exactly what he had said.

"Well, I'd say turn yourself in and trust the judicial system, I mean that's the right thing to do, but after what I've read here. . . ." He nodded to the paper, and looked at her. "I don't know. They've got a witness, and probably prints and everything. Looks like a lock, and this Hill guy is . . ."

"Yes, thanks for reminding me."

"Sorry." He sat up grabbed the coffee press and split the dregs into their cups. "So, if you don't want to turn yourself in, I figure," he ruminated, "you've got maybe two shots. One: just try to save yourself. Come with me to the Bahamas and wait for this all to blow over."

She mused the word "Bahamas," out loud.

"No problems mon." Dan started a little grin, but it faltered. "Sun, sand, crystal clear water, cozy little anchorages, lobster . . ."

"Just me and you?" That was one scary idea.

"Just you and me."

"Run away?"

"Gone with the wind."

"And you'd be willing to do that?"

"Why not?"

"That's pretty crazy. Are you really that desperate, Dan? Run away with a fugitive? You don't even know me."

Dan shrugged. "You seem nice."

"And this isn't going to blow over."

"No," Dan agreed, no longer smiling. "Probably not for a long, long time."

"So, what's the other idea?"

"Well, this is the really crazy one." He looked at her, looked away and then back again. "We figure out a way to prove you're innocent."

"Prove my innocence," she scoffed. "Yeah, right. How?"

Dan shrugged. "Beats me. I'm not Sam Spade here." He shrugged again. "Find the real murderer? I don't know. You're the one that knows everything. I just read the paper, that's all I've got."

That thought hung in the air until the VHF radio

squawked. "*Vitamin Sea, Vitamin Sea*, this is *Windsong* on sixteen."

The interruption irritated Teri, but Dan was interested. He stood up, and when they switched channels he followed.

Someone said, "Morning Tony, how was your night?"

"Pretty exciting. It's some girl they're looking for—she murdered T J Hill."

"A young girl. Isn't that something?"

"I think his house is the big peachy-looking job right behind us. Still a couple of police cars there. They think she drowned."

Dan was peering out the companionway. He looked at the shore. He checked the other boats at anchor. There was a police boat by the big peach-colored house.

On the radio they kept chatting. "They've got divers coming."

"I hate to miss it, but we're planning to take this window."

"Lucaya? We're thinking of that too."

"Lucaya or the Berries. I'd like to push all the way to Nassau, but Mary isn't ready. We'll see. *Alpaca Promise* is about five miles out, not in the stream yet, but they say the seas are about two feet, smooth and wide apart. Not bad at all. *Skeedaddle* and *Sea Gypsy* are getting ready."

"Looks like we've got our raging calm. When are you going?"

"Getting ready now. But say Malcolm, *Alpaca Promise* also reports they're searching every boat leaving the inlet, so if you've got the young lady on board, watch out."

"I wish. Look, I'm going to call Dan, you know Dan on *Red Line*. He wants to cross."

Teri pointed at him. *"Red Line?"* she mouthed.

Dan held up one finger. "Break, break, this is Dan here. I've been reading the mail. Looks good, but I don't think I'll be crossing today."

"Why, Dan? You have that young lady on board?"

Dan responded by saying, "She's a babe, isn't she? I got the paper this morning, nice photo. But, I think I'll pick up that wind generator we were talking about. I'll catch the next window and see you all down the line."

After finishing up the formalities Dan hung up the mike and punched the radio back to channel sixteen. "Looks like getting to the Bahamas might be a problem. Maybe in a few days things will—"

"They won't."

"Naw, I guess they won't." He began to put away the groceries. "In the meantime we should figure out a way to prove you're innocent."

"Okey-dokey," she mocked him. She'd read the papers, and she knew she hadn't killed anyone, but she still felt guilty.

"What have you got to lose by trying? Not much." He scrunched the empty plastic bags into a ball. "Besides, I'd hate to think that the real murderer is going to get away. I get the feeling no one is looking for anybody except you."

Hill's wide eyes were back in her mind. *That's true,* she thought. *It wouldn't be right for the real murderer to get away.*

Dan watched the other boats leave. Then he cranked over the big diesel. It caught and shook for a moment before it settled down. He eased the throttle back, put the engine into forward for a short burst, then slipped it into neutral. As the boat coasted ahead, he loped along the side deck. He grabbed the anchor rope and hand-over-hand hauled it in. *Red Line* began to twist and drift sideways with the tide. He secured the anchor and casually sauntered back into the cockpit, glancing over at the police boats and divers still working close to shore.

He put *Red Line* in gear and increased the throttle. Eyeing his depth, Dan wound his way out to the main channel of the Intra-Coastal Waterway. There he could turn south, and head for the inlet, the ocean and the Bahamas. That was tempting, but he reluctantly turned north. This section of the waterway was narrow, the banks heavily developed, and the channel passed under a number of Bascule bridges, so to be safe Teri stayed out of sight below.

She finished up the dishes then came and sat on the bottom of the companionway steps. "You've never done this sort of thing before?" Beneath her the diesel engine thumped out its slow monotonous rhythm.

"What?"

"What would you call it, detective work?"

"No, never."

"I mean, what makes you think we can figure out a way to prove I'm innocent?"

"Never said we could." He shrugged. "All I said was, you might want to take a crack at it. Nothing to lose."

"I guess." She didn't sound enthusiastic.

"We've got one big thing going for us."

"What's that?"

"You're innocent, right?"

Teri answered, "I am innocent. I didn't kill Mr. Hill."

She repeated it over and over to herself, like a mantra. It didn't make her feel any more confident.

She gazed about. She wanted to go on deck—he'd mentioned there were dolphins playing beside the boat and she really wanted to see them. Instead, while she was rinsing out her clothes from the night before and finding places to hang them to dry, she had roamed around the inside of the boat. It was like a tube, not much wider than the width of her arms, but long. You entered the cabin by coming down the companionway stairs. On the right was the head of the quarter berth, and the rest of the bed curled back into a cave under the cockpit. On the left was the u-shaped galley, with an ice box, a stove in the middle under a port window, and the sink. The main cabin in the center of the boat had only a drop leaf table, with settee bench seats running lengthwise on either side. There was very little actual floor space. Further forward, wedged into a nook on the left was the tiny head, then on the right at the bow was the fore peak. That's where she found boxes of textbooks, books such as: *Introduction to Psychology, Modes of Reasoning, Classic Philosophy*. The pages of all the books were crisp and new, as if they'd never been opened.

While she sat, he stood in the cockpit above her and steered. Dan's boat had a tiller. Sometimes he steered using a hiking stick so that he could sit far out to one side on the edge of the cockpit and lean back against the lifelines. Now, to be closer to Teri, he stood with the tiller between his knees.

She watched, then asked, "So, what are you doing here?"

"Me?"

"Yes. Shouldn't you be at work or something? Don't you have a job?"

"Long story," he answered, "off topic. We've got to focus."

Teri nodded. *He was right, of course. They had to concentrate on proving her innocence, but how? Where to start?*

She watched him for a while, then announced with a shake of her head, "You are one peculiar man."

"Thanks."

"Thanks?"

"Well, do you mean peculiar good, or peculiar bad?"

"I don't know, just peculiar."

"Well, I don't know if that deserves a thanks or not, but I'll stick with thanks."

"Why thanks?"

"Why not? Peculiar could mean interesting, I'll take it that way. How's that? Interesting is good, don't you think?"

Teri didn't know if interesting was good or bad. "How did you end up here on a sailboat?"

"You mean why am I not working nine-to-five, with two point three kids and a mortgage?"

"Yes, I guess."

"You mean did I ever have a job, and why am I—still a fairly young fellow—not working as a responsible member of society?"

"Yes."

"Hmm, good question." There was a roar and he glanced back over his shoulder. "But I'm not sure I have a simple answer for that. And really, it's not terribly important, and were way off topic here." Then he muttered, "Boat."

Teri ducked down.

A moment later the sailboat rocked in the wake of a sportfisherman. It roared past them like a race car, and the wake hit. Teri was tossed across the cabin—she bounced off a counter and floundered into the berth. Dishes, pots and pans crashed everywhere. Dan didn't seem to notice. He kept steering.

Teri waited until the violent rocking died down again, then she took up her seat on the companionway steps. She had picked up a pad of paper that had fallen from the shelf above the bed. She found a pen.

Dan saw her and smiled. "Now we're getting somewhere." He laughed. "Okay, let's brainstorm."

"How about some coffee?" Teri suggested.

They sipped more coffee. They finished off the cinnamon buns. They nibbled on cookies.

"What have we got so far?"

Teri announced, "A sugar overdose?" She smiled. She'd been eating all morning, but still she felt peckish. Frustration was building up inside her. She was craving some master stroke, some brilliant spark of inspiration that could give her hope, but there was no spark, nothing. "Let's face it, we don't know how to do this."

He seemed to give the idea serious consideration. "Right now, we've got some time." Dan danced a little to one side as the boat turned. He checked.

Teri wrote, *Goal: to prove Teri Peterson didn't murder T J Hill.*

"Good work," Dan enthused.

Teri looked at what she had written. It had taken an hour

to come up with it. She muttered, "Hopeless," then added, "First spot you can, take us ashore. I'll turn myself in."

She was shocked when he nodded. She wondered who he was and how he ended up here, but she knew it was an 'off topic.' Again she wondered how she had fallen into this predicament. She felt guilty and ashamed and had to keep reminding herself *I'm innocent. I didn't kill Mr. Hill. I've done nothing wrong. I'm innocent.* Finally she announced, "We are *way* out of our league here."

Something painful flushed through Dan, she could see it. He murmured, "Yeah, but . . ." He concentrated on steering then shrugged and said, "Maybe we should hire a professional."

"Maybe. But that takes money."

"Don't worry about money."

"Don't worry about money? You've got money? Are you rich?" She regretted being so blunt, but she had to know.

"I figure money should be the least of your worries, so just don't worry about money, okay?"

"Yes, but do you have money? Because I don't."

"I think I have enough money, yes."

Teri looked at him again. They could be talking about a *lot* of money. "I'll pay you back." *Somehow,* she thought. She didn't know how, but she didn't say that out loud.

He gave her a distracted nod as he turned the boat again and altered course.

For Teri, there was a certain appeal about giving up, removing the uncertainty, getting it over with. She was willing to work hard and fight, but how? The frustration of not knowing what to do was the problem. Despite surging energy and feverish brain activity, she didn't know where to direct it . . . she was just flailing about in ignorance. She wanted to scream. She was in agony.

"This isn't so bad, is it?" Dan said. "I mean right here, right now, the moment."

Warm sunshine streamed in the ports and hatches. The sailboat kept chugging along relentlessly. The moment was pleasant enough, but she couldn't block out the creeping anxiety, the need to make some sort of progress. She wanted to get far away, and it felt like they were going so slowly. She wanted to figure out who really murdered Hill, and in that respect they were getting nowhere at all.

Dan added, "I'll bet a lot of Canadians would trade their snow-shovels to be here and just sit in the sun."

"Well, maybe I can find a Canadian woman to trade places with." She stared at him, waiting for the slow little grin she knew would come. He was wearing sunglasses, so she could no longer see his eyes, but there it was—the cheeks barely rising. Twelve hours ago she didn't even know him. But twelve hours ago seemed like another lifetime.

Dan checked his watch. He looked at the chart book and slowed the boat almost to a stop, then he threw the tiller over and the boat began a tight circle.

"Bridge ahead," he said. "Doesn't open again for twenty minutes."

"So what do we do?"

"We wait."

"Wait? We just sit and float here for twenty minutes?"

He nodded.

Teri groaned.

*   *   *

Dan lashed the tiller and hopped down below. He dug out a floppy hat and a pair of sunglasses. He dropped the hat on Teri's head and handed her the shades. He bounded back on deck and unlashed the tiller, bringing the boat's keel back into the narrow, deep water channel.

Teri put on the glasses and followed him up on deck. There were no boats or houses in sight, no people at all. The shore was near on both sides. Fingers of mangrove swamp reached out to them.

"Okay, there," he said, pointing at the little stern ripple that the boat was making. "Watch."

Dutifully Teri stood and looked down at the shimmering water. "This is slow," she said. The sailboat puttered along, not creating the slightest breeze. "Is this as fast as we can go?"

"Top speed."

"I could walk faster than this."

"Almost. The pace of life on a sailboat takes a little getting used to. Quite . . ."

"Slow?" she suggested.

"Yeah, slow, that's it."

"How do you get anywhere going this slow? Isn't it frustrating? You came all the way down from Canada at this pace?"

"Yeah."

"You know you could have flown here in a couple of hours."

"But I might have missed something."

Suddenly there was a gasp at her feet. Teri looked down and saw the silvery-blue face of a dolphin staring right into her eyes. She could hear him suck fresh air back in through his blow hole. The dolphin seemed to smirk before it dove again. A smaller dolphin, following by its side, did the same.

Dan's cheeks rose into a smile. He spoke deliberately, pausing between each thought, "I saw them once. The parent dolphins were throwing the babies up into the air, like they were juggling them. And they were making those dolphin noises, like they were laughing, like it was a party game or something."

Teri smiled. "I'd love to see that."

"It was early in the morning. The sun was just barely up, the water was flat and calm and they were in a little cove on the side of the waterway." Dan laughed. "I've only seen that once. I keep watching, hoping to catch them doing it again."

Teri had to admit that the moment, right here, right now, was nice and peaceful. The thin bow of the sailboat cut slowly but easily through the glassy water. The boat seemed content to merge into the tranquility.

Dan handed her back the pad and pen. "I think we can handle both watching for dolphins and brainstorming. Let's try it from a different viewpoint. What proof do they have?"

They each sat on opposite sides of the cockpit looking at each other. Teri spoke as she wrote, "Weapon, fingerprints, opportunity. Probably lots of physical evidence like blood and hair, maybe even DNA. And an eyewitness."

"Good," Dan enthused. "Now we're cooking." He glanced over at the shoreline, up to the depth sounder, then down at the chart and back to Teri. He did this several times.

"Why is that good?" Teri lamented. "That isn't good. They have enough physical evidence to convince anyone that I killed Hill. I mean, *I* know I didn't, but I still feel all this guilt. I have to keep reminding myself that I didn't do it. We aren't doing good here at all."

"Understatement." Dan laughed.

"And I wish you wouldn't laugh." When she glared at him he wilted, and she felt bad.

His eyes made another round trip. Pushing the hiking stick brought *Red Line* back into the channel. "Any motive?" he asked.

"No," Teri answered. "I didn't have any reason to kill Mr. Hill. I didn't even know him, at least not well. I had just started working there."

"No motive at all?"

"None."

"Well, there's something."

"I guess."

"*Somebody* killed him. They must have had a motive."

"Sure, but what?"

"Politician: must have had scads of enemies." Dan continued pondering out loud. "Senator. Presidential candidate," he'd read that in the paper, "is that a motive?"

"What? The Democrats killed him? They don't kill opposition candidates."

"Don't they? No, I guess not."

"They just dredge up dirt and crucify them."

"Maybe they couldn't find any dirt. Paper said this guy was a saint."

Teri nodded. She spoke with sorrow. "He did seem like a nice man."

"But still a politician, right?" His voice was gentle, thoughtful. "Must have had lots of enemies. Rich, successful—half the world hates this guy."

Teri frowned. "I suppose, but . . ."

"He must have had at least one serious enemy, and they had to have a reason."

"Dan, I appreciate all you're trying to do, but I'm not some hard-nosed private investigator. I'm just a nanny."

No more dolphins broke the surface. She watched a blue heron standing tall and motionless in the shallows. Then she continued, "It was only a temporary thing. I took a semester off from school to earn some money. Thought I was lucky to find such a neat job." That thought hung in the air before she added, "I'm taking early childhood education. I saw your text books down there—are you taking a correspondence course? Psychology?"

Dan didn't respond.

Teri looked down at the forgotten piece of paper. It was hopeless. Even Dan was looking beaten. She said, "I'll write down exactly what really happened, how's that?"

He mulled it over. "Yeah, that's good. We can also put down what they say happened, and compare."

"Perhaps. But I was thinking that I would write what really happened—everything I know—and send a copy to the police and the papers, and maybe it will help prove my innocence."

"Hey. That's not half bad. That's very good."

Teri began to write.

She hadn't gotten far when Dan interrupted. "Except right now they're searching the bottom of the lake. They think you might be dead. Maybe that would be better—maybe they'll stop looking."

"Yes, but they aren't going to find my body."

They talked it over and decided she should write out her version of what happened and they would decide later how best to use it.

At marker number "19" Dan slowed down the engine, then slipped it into neutral. A slick black cormorant rose out of the nest atop the marker pole and spread his wings to dry.

They were barely moving; keeping just enough momentum to keep going. He swung the tiller and eased out of the channel, heading into a small lagoon. He went up to the foredeck, dropped anchor, and gave the motor a burst of reverse, and turned it off.

The world was suddenly very still. There were no other boats, no houses, roads, cars, or people. Teri could smell the ocean. Through a veil of short trees and tall grass she could see white sand—a thin strip of dunes separated the waterway from the ocean. Her impression of Florida was crowded beaches, crowded highways, crowded amusement parks . . . an endless hubbub of people, stores and automobiles. This idyllic spot was empty and quiet.

Teri had made a fruit salad for lunch. Dan read her notes while he ate. They sat on either side of the cockpit, feet flat, backs against the cabin, facing the stern. Abruptly, he stopped reading. "Just a second. You saw the murder?"

"I was there. I saw the end—sort of."

"Let me see if I've got this straight. You witnessed the actual murder, the real murder?"

"Sort of."

"Sort of?"

"I mean, I saw the guy running away."

"The guy?"

"Yes, I think it was a guy."

"There you go. We've just eliminated half the people on the planet. Old guy? Young guy?"

"I don't know."

"Big, small?"

"No."

"Fat? Thin?"

"Average, I think."

"This is great, really great. Write all this down. We've eliminated a few billion people here."

"Great, what's that leave? A few billion more?"

"Yeah, that's all. And it's not the wife, right? We can eliminate the wife?"

"I think so."

"But you're not sure?"

"Well, ninety percent sure. I mean I don't think it was her . . . but I'm not sure. It was dark and hectic. I saw the back of the person running away. At first I didn't know what was happening. I didn't look at the person escaping, I was more concerned with Mr. Hill. I saw him on the floor and went right over to him. I didn't think about anything else."

Dan nodded. He kept reading, but gradually his excitement drained away and he became very quiet. He dropped the pages down below into the safety of the cabin. "Teri, I didn't know it was so . . ." He waited a moment, then added, "Must have been terrible."

It snuck up on her. She'd been eating grapes and watching a snowy white egret meandering through the shallows, and as he spoke it all burst back into her mind, and she wasn't prepared to fend off the vision. Squeezing her eyes shut didn't help, and she struggled to hold back tears. She wrapped her arms tightly across her chest. It was too late. Her chest started to heave and she burst into tears.

Somehow she found herself nestled in his arms, her head on his shoulder, and she just let go and cried. She felt if she could cry long enough and hard enough she'd be able to awaken from this dream and the horrible memories would be gone, washed away in the flood of tears.

Chapter Three

T he sandpiper tipped at the waist and repeatedly nipped into the ripple of the receding tide. A second later, head down, shoulders hunched, feet scurrying, the little bird raced up the rise of the beach, retreating just before a fresh wave surged.

Teri stood still. The warm water lapped up around her ankles, then sank away. The white sand sank between her toes. She was feeling better: something about the slow ceaseless undulations of the ocean managed to massage her mind and caress her soul. She'd be content to stand in the sun and the gentle surf forever. As long as she didn't think she was fine, but every time she allowed her mind to roam, even this peaceful sanctuary was invaded. It was well and good to try to enjoy the moment, and sometimes she could forget her dilemma and enjoy a frolicking dolphin, or the warm sun on her face, but reality was always looming in the background. Her world had gone crazy—she was suddenly a hunted criminal. But it couldn't be true, how could this have happened?

"Now what?" Teri snapped.

Dan was at her side. He glanced over. "Swim?" he suggested.

Before she could stop herself Teri released a snort of derision. Then she scowled at him, but he only smiled a little and said, "Can't swim? I know you can swim."

"I haven't a suit."

"Oh, oh right. But, there's no one—I mean, you could. People do. No. No, of course not."

She wore her hair tucked up under the big sun hat, the cavernous Maple Leaf T-shirt, and sweat pants rolled up to her knees. She looked at him in disbelief, then suddenly realizing he was up to his usual tricks she snickered and rolled her eyes.

"What?" Dan asked.

"I didn't say anything." She ventured out into the deeper water.

He didn't follow her. He stood and watched her walking away. "I know lots of girls who would, in a situation like this—"

She knew he was teasing her, shocking her, distracting her from her real predicament. For once she'd like to shock him. What would he do if she did suddenly shuck the baggy clothes and charge out into the surf? Teri glanced up and down the shore. He wouldn't be shocked, she knew that. He wasn't like her—nothing shocked Dan. He'd shuck his clothes and join in, and he'd have that slow, devilish little grin that you had to check real close to detect—the one that started in his eyes and never really caught hold of his mouth.

Far in the distance two people meandered around the curve of the beach: an older couple, heads down looking for shells.

Dan called to her, "What size are you?"

"Why?"

"I'll go get you some new clothes. I mean you really need a bathing suit, this is Florida. I'll run into town."

"I don't trust you to pick out clothes for me. Especially not a swim suit."

"Oh." Dan stopped and started again. "Guess I can understand that. Do you want to drop by the mall later and pick out some new togs?"

"Togs?"

"Or do you want to keep wearing this stuff? I mean, I like the look of you in my old clothes. I have no problems with that and I have lots of clothes, but . . ."

"Fine." She sort of liked it too. His baggy clothes were like camouflage—camouflage from her pursuers, camouflage from him, camouflage from her previous self. The alien clothes made her feel like she was living someone else's life, that the real Teri Peterson was still in the nursery wearing pretty clothes and reading stories to the Hill children, and she was just pretending to be somebody else: a fugitive, a murderer on the run.

The shell seekers were getting closer, but they didn't look up from their beach combing. If they were undercover cops they had the best disguises ever—well-tanned and chubby. Teri yanked the sweat pants up to the top of her thighs. She faced out to sea and took a few more steps.

Dan turned and waved a greeting to the couple as they passed. Then Dan and Teri curved back into the shallows, walking side by side.

Then a jogger appeared, and as they watched several more people began to pop up, all ostensibly out for an afternoon stroll. Dan and Teri retreated back to the seclusion of the boat.

"You know," Teri said thoughtfully, "I really think I should send that letter."

Dan nodded in agreement.

"If something were to happen to me, I'd like my version of things to be heard, even if nobody believes it. And I don't want people to think I've drowned. I don't want to just get away, with people believing I'm a murderer. Somehow I'd like to prove my innocence."

"So we go on the offensive."

"What?" she scoffed. "What offensive?"

"We get your story out, hire a lawyer. What else?"

Teri thought about it. "Maybe hire a real detective— somebody who knows how to handle this. Is that okay?"

"Absolutely. I'll drop you back at the boat, then I'll run a few errands."

"We can't do this ourselves. I mean, I don't know how. If I could get to a library, or access the internet I could do some research, but . . ."

As they began to cut across the rise in the center of the barrier key, Teri could see new masts sprouting in the anchorage. She looked at Dan.

"Company," he muttered. They walked slowly, moving up above the tide line to a path through the sea oats. Their feet sank deep into the soft white sand.

Three sailboats surrounded *Red Line*. Once they were close enough to discern the shape and color of the hulls, Dan said, "I know all of these people. They're all friends I've made along the way. I guess that's good, but they'll want to have a pot luck dinner or happy hour, or some sort of get together. I don't think I can just leave you here on the boat. They'll come by, and want to chat. Just to be neighborly."

Teri felt relieved. "That's okay. I'll run the errands with you. I don't think I can handle being alone anyway."

One boat was still in the process of anchoring. A thin white-haired man stood on the bow, pointing and yelling instructions to his wife at the helm. The woman, equally thin and white-haired, wasn't noticing her husband's exhortations—she had spied Dan on the shore. She was waving. The husband shouted, then shook his head and made angry violent motions with his arms. The wife ignored him: She was still waving, furiously trying to get Dan's attention. Dan smiled and returned the wave.

Dan and Teri yanked the dinghy off the shore into the water. Dan pretended not to notice any of the neighbors beckoning him over and zipped his dinghy straight to the stern of *Red Line*. Teri scampered up the ladder, then down below into the cabin. Dan stepped into the cockpit. He leaned on the boom and carried on a conversation across the water with Neville and Helen from *Carpe Diem*. He deftly confined the discussion to the fine weather and how long it might last.

Doors locked, windows down a crack: Teri sat and waited patiently like a well-trained family dog. On the floor at her feet lay the messy remains of a sandwich and two big shopping bags on the seat beside her. Dan had shopped fast. He shopped for clothes the way he shopped for groceries: grab some of everything. It took barely fifteen minutes: T-shirts, polo shirts, cotton shorts, one pair of khaki slacks, jeans, sneakers, six bathing suits.

All in all, she had to admit, he hadn't done too bad. Then again, fugitives can't be fussy.

This was the last stop. The sun was setting behind the tall manicured palm trees and the pastel strip malls. There was a steady stream of traffic out on the highway, but the distant corner of the parking lot was empty.

Dan had visited a lawyer, stopping in at the first sign he had chanced upon. A woman named Anne Grant had spoken to him. Teri found comfort in the fact that she was a woman—perhaps a female lawyer would be more sympathetic to another woman's plight. According to Dan, Ms. Grant had offered some preliminary advice. First, Teri should turn herself in, immediately. It would look better and she'd be safer. Secondly, if Teri chose to turn herself in, the chances for bail were 'virtually nil, but we will try our best.' Ms. Grant said that she had been following the story, and yes, there *did* seem to be an overwhelming amount of evidence.

Dan faxed a copy of Teri's story to a phone number in Toronto. He included a cover letter instructing his agent to send copies to 'every police force and news desk in Florida, and another copy to Anne Grant.'

He was now in the office of a private investigator. Teri sat slouched down in the back of the van, staring at the windshield, with nary a thought floating through her mind.

Her mind was numb, it felt like it was taking a well-deserved nap—a respite from the emotional contortions it had recently been subjected to. She continued to stare until a flicker of movement nearby spooked her, and she turned and saw him lope over the little green shrubs and oleanders that divided up the aisles of parking spaces. She reached forward and unlocked the door. Dan slipped into the driver's seat.

"So?" she asked as she settled once more into the back.

Dan started the engine. "It went much the same as it did with the lawyer: I'm just a concerned citizen, I know Ms. Peterson, but not well." He put the car in reverse and began to back up. "I don't believe she had any reason to murder Mr. Hill, nor was she capable of it, and I want them to work on her behalf."

"And they bought it?"

"Oh, probably not, but that's not important. Both the lawyer and the investigator said they didn't know exactly what they could do, but they each took the retainer and said they would look into it. I'm supposed to get back to them in a couple of days." He turned north on the highway. "He seemed like a nice enough guy. Sounded like he knew his stuff," Dan added in an attempt to cheer her up.

In fact the detective, Clay Hedoby, was enthusiastic about taking such a high profile case. He explained he was an ex-member of the local police force, so he claimed to have good connections there. Dan asked him to find out everything he could about Hill, who was in the house that night, and compile list of other potential murderers. Dan told Teri all of this.

They had actually accomplished very little, but it was a

start and a lot more than she would have dreamt possible. Teri thought about that for a while, then changed her mind. He—Dan—had done everything: rented the van, chosen the clothes, bought the lunch, visited the lawyer and the investigators, came up with the stories to tell, and paid for everything. It was Dan who had suggested first sending the fax to Toronto from a corner store, and then to re-fax her story to the police and the papers, hoping it might confuse her pursuers into thinking she had made it far away. All the while Teri had sat there in the van as useful as the family pooch.

She crept forward, up between the seats. Their eyes met in the rear view mirror. Teri hesitated and for a moment they gazed at each other until Dan broke away to stop for a light.

Teri turned from the mirror. She leaned toward him, and suddenly it all felt bizarre—the faraway man in the mirror was close and warm and real. A cool kiss on the cheek felt like a lot more than just a little peck. She kissed him near his ear and the curve of his jaw, but it didn't feel right and Dan seemed to shrink away. He seemed more focused on the traffic than ever, even though the light was just changing to green. Suddenly feeling flushed and embarrassed Teri sank into the front seat beside him.

"Thanks," she announced, her voice too loud, then she added, "Thanks for everything."

The van began to move. He glanced over at her.

She added, "You know, for all the . . . everything you're doing."

Dan nodded. He focused on driving the van. The sun had

set and the salmon colored sky was fading into a deep un-
dulating lavender.

Teri could still feel the whiskers prickling her lips. "You
should shave," she muttered.

"I should," he spoke slowly, very subdued. He changed
lanes. He ran his hand over his chin. "Yes, I should shave,
especially if that is going to become a habit."

Teri snickered and shook her head. "I wouldn't count on
it." For the rest of the journey she made a point of not
looking at him, but she couldn't avoid thinking about him.

The rubber dinghy nudged the hull. The dinghy was tied
at the stern of the sailboat and drifted on the unseen cur-
rents, occasionally wandering around and nudging up
against *Red Line*, like a calf nuzzling it's mother. At first,
the noise gave Teri a start, but gradually she got used to
it, just like she grew accustomed to the boat suddenly toppling back and forth in a wake.

Dan was spending a long time brushing his teeth. From
her new bunk in the fore peak she could hear him in the
washroom, "the head," as he called it. She wondered if he
would come in to say goodnight. A moment later he rapped
on the door.

"Yes?"

Hunched over, he poked his head and shoulders in. "You
going to be okay in here? We can switch if you like."

"You don't fit in here." The fore peak had a thin berth
on either side of the hull, V shaped, coming to a point right
at the bow of the boat: sort of claustrophobic, sort of cozy.
Teri was on one side, stretched out beneath her blanket.
Dan crouched and, hunched up like a pretzel, he managed

to sit on the other side. But his head had to bend forward almost to his chest, and he ended up lying on the port bunk.

"It's smaller than a prison cell." She laughed. "But I like it. I'll be fine."

He nodded.

It was the books she had noticed when they were cleaning up the fore peak, more of those new textbooks. Confronted, he had admitted he was taking university correspondence courses. He seemed defensive about it and Teri let it drop.

"Teri, tell me more about the house, the security, the layout. Who was there that night?"

"No one really. There was no special security that I noticed, I mean he wasn't President yet, he didn't even have the nomination."

"So anyone could have dropped in, killed him, and fled?"

She stared at the ceiling. They both lay on their backs and stared at the white vinyl ceiling. "As far as I know. Either they had to be lucky though, or they knew the place pretty well. There were always a lot of people around. There was a big garage, maybe three car, that had been turned into—they called it "the pit." Sort of the campaign office, with rows of tables, chairs, phones, televisions, portable partition things, computers, all that stuff. People worked in there around the clock, sometimes dozens of people."

"How many people were there that night?"

"I have no idea."

"And where was Hill killed?"

"In his study. He had two studies, or private offices. One was in the house, upstairs off of his bedroom, the other down between the house and the garage." She took a deep breath. "He was killed in the upstairs study."

"So the killer had to walk through the house?"

"Yes. Up the stairs to the study."

"Was that a common thing?"

"No, you learned quickly that household business was dealt with in the upstairs study. You know, personal stuff, anything having to do with the family. You know what I mean?"

She didn't see him but felt his nod. They were only a couple of feet apart.

"And political affairs were taken care of in the office downstairs. I never really went down there, and those people, the political advisors and all, rarely came up. It was two separate worlds. Mr. Hill was the only one who belonged in both. Even Mrs. Hill didn't often venture down into the pit."

"She wasn't involved in the political end of things?"

"No. She avoided it. She told me sometimes she felt selfish and guilty, but she preferred life when he was an anonymous teacher. They were both high school teachers when they met."

Teri thought for a second. "Occasionally political people, especially his close advisors, would go in the main house, but they'd stand out. You'd always sort of wonder what they were doing, and if something important was happening."

"But someone could go upstairs."

"Sure."

"And they could have the night Hill was murdered."

"Yes."

"Without anyone seeing them?"

"I guess so . . . there was no security that I knew of. Hypothetically anybody could have wandered in and not been noticed, even from the street. The side door into the pit was always open."

"But whoever it was must have known where they were going."

"Yes, probably . . . but not necessarily. Who knows?"

"And you went in there because . . . ?"

"I wanted to find out when I was going to be paid. The next day—that would be today—was my day off. Karen, Mrs. Hill, told me the checks had all been made out, but Mr. Hill still had to sign them."

"Maybe tomorrow you could draw a layout of the house." Dan paused. He yawned then asked, "Where could the murderer have escaped to when you came into the study?"

"He went out onto the balcony, that's all I know. From there he could go anywhere. The balcony runs along the back of the house. There are stairs to the ground, and other doors back into the house."

"They could have come in there too?"

"If a door was open."

"And where was Mrs. Hill?"

"As far as I know she was in the master bedroom, but I don't—"

"Right beside the study?"

"Yes, that's the master bedroom. But I can only assume she was in there. She might actually have been up with the kids, or . . ." The boat rocked. A moment later she could hear the waves lapping up against the nearby bank. Stretching her legs, she inadvertently nudged his feet with hers. The shape of the vee berth, coming to a narrow point, forced their feet together. That was nice, it was comforting to feel his touch. She remembered sharing the bunk the night before and wondered if he was going to spend the night. It'd be okay. She wouldn't mind him sleeping beside her, feet together. She was afraid of being alone.

Dan rolled onto his side and looked over at her.

Teri spoke. "Believe me, I've thought this all through, and it doesn't lead anywhere. I don't know who killed Mr. Hill, and I don't know how we can possibly find out."

He looked at her openly for the longest time. She felt a kiss in the air, and she wondered what she would do if he leaned over from his bunk, leaned across the narrow gulf that separated them and . . . she didn't know what would happen. She didn't know if she would shriek in terror or swoon, or just go brain dead from emotional overload.

Nodding, he swung his legs out of the bunk, "That's because you're not a killer, so you can't think like a killer. Since you can't think of any reason to kill anyone, you can't possibly figure out who may have killed Mr. Hill. But somebody did. Somebody had a reason that was compelling enough and made sense to them."

"Like what?"

"I don't know . . . it would have to be important though. I don't know. I wouldn't make a good killer either, I'm afraid. We have to think more like killers."

He stood. The lack of headroom in the tiny cabin kept him bent over like a hunchback, his head down close to hers. He touched her shoulder with his hand. "You okay? Are you going to be able to sleep?"

"I think so. I feel tired enough."

"Good. Me too." She felt his hand innocently caress her shoulder, like a father saying goodnight to a daughter. "If there is anything you need, anything I can do, just holler."

He turned off the light and the cabin door clicked shut. He was gone. Teri was alone, felt very alone, and wondered why he hadn't tried to kiss her. And what would she have done if he did? She could hear him rustling out of his clothes and pulling back a sheet not twenty feet away. She felt abandoned. He had patted her on the shoulder!

She was angry with herself for even thinking the thoughts, but she kept thinking. In the van, he had recoiled from her innocent peck on his cheek, like he had been stung by a bee. They were alone in a small boat and he suggested she could sleep in her own cabin. Her body was weary, but her brain kept racing. Why did she care? If she must lay awake thinking she should concentrate on who killed Mr. Hill. Up until now she'd been coasting—*he'd* been the one doing all the work, *thinking,* trying his best. It was time for her to get involved in helping to save herself. But she didn't know who killed him and she didn't like to replay the murder in her mind.

Dark, quiet . . . it was eerie in the fore peak. Only dim starlight seeped down through the small hatch.

She couldn't sleep. His appearance intrigued her. He was tall and rugged and, despite what appeared to be a lazy indolent lifestyle and a healthy appetite, he was lean and muscular. He wasn't desperate—he didn't need her. He was handsome, in an intense, sort of a frightening way, but paradoxically he seemed good, kind and easy going. For all his peculiar mannerisms, he was intelligent, financially secure and generous. Just because she was scared of him didn't mean lots of women weren't attracted to his type. He didn't need her at all. She was only trouble. He didn't need her; *she* needed *him*. And she had to admit it was cozier in that other berth, than here alone. Amazingly, she wasn't scared when he was near—like she felt now.

Teri was almost asleep when the dinghy bumped once more against the hull. She rolled over and ground her head into the pillow.

Again she thought of him leaning over, leaning over to her and kissing her. She thought about that for awhile, and thought about what her reaction might be, and what his reaction would be, until finally she decided it was probably for the best that he hadn't.

There was a footstep on the deck. It was soft and quiet: Dan's considerate footstep. He probably didn't want to wake her. Then another step—but different somehow—and she wondered if it really was Dan up there creeping around on deck.

Chapter Four

Teri grasped the door handle. She turned it, twisting the chrome lever down until it stopped, and began to push the door open, slowly.

She listened but heard nothing, nothing beyond the resounding thunder of her heart. The main cabin was a confusion of dull shadows. Leaning forward, Teri shifted her weight, ounce by ounce.

The companionway hatch was still closed, and that erased any lingering hope that the footsteps on deck might be Dan's. She took another step. As she watched, the companionway hatch began to creep open. Time had run out. Whoever was out there was on their way in. She had to warn Dan. She took two quick steps towards his bunk. The boards squeaked beneath her feet. The hatch stopped moving. She froze.

A gentle hand touched her wrist; warm and close upon

her ear, a silent, "Shhh." A shudder flared and died at the base of her spine. Her shoulders tingled. Dan released her.

Then the hatch started to slide again. Abruptly it stopped with a clunk. The companionway was locked. She could hear mumbling. A click, a flashlight, a sliver of dull yellow appeared and darted into the cabin. Someone was trying to figure out how the hatch was fastened, and how it could be opened.

Dan and Teri retreated into the fore peak. He sat on the bunk, reached up and eased open the hatch. Unlike the companionway hatch, this one flipped up like a hinged lid. Dan waited, listening, then raised his head through the opening. Teri grabbed some clothes. Again he paused and, silent as a cloud, he drifted up and out and onto the deck. A moment later, he reached down and took her hand. Teri kneeled up onto the bunk, her head and shoulders protruding through the small aperture. Using her arms she hoisted up her legs, and lay flat, hugging the deck, cowering behind the coach roof.

Everything was shockingly still and quiet. The water was like black, luminous glass. The stars were scattered smudges hidden behind a creamy haze.

She took a breath and raised her head. She peeked at the stern. Two shadows were hunched in the cockpit. One man turned and slunk down behind the dodger, then she saw him again. He was getting something out of his dinghy—a long thin tool.

She glanced back to Dan, but he had vanished. He had moved so quickly and quietly she hadn't even noticed. She turned. She saw the glow of his eyes at the lip of the deck.

He was over the edge, hanging onto the side. His legs had to be in the water, but she heard nothing.

Back in the cockpit the two big shadows were starting to stand. They were wiggling the skinny tool into the hatch. They pushed on it and it cracked. The hatch was being pried up like the lid on a can of paint.

Teri slithered over the side. Dan moved slowly. He merged with the water making nary a ripple. She heard the companionway hatch fly back. She slipped into the water, ready to swim, but Dan held her back. He edged back along the hull of the boat, back to the stern and the intruders' dinghy. He held her hand and put it on the rubber gunnel, then Dan reached up and carefully untied the dinghy. Immediately and silently it drifted away on the tidal current.

The lights went on in *Red Line*. The ports glowed like yellow eyes. One of the men came back on deck. Dan slithered up into the dinghy, and Teri did the same. Looking back she saw someone on the fore deck probing the darkness with a flashlight.

The night remained eerily quiet.

The flashlight began to trace along the shore. Dan prepped the motor.

She could hear two men whispering, but couldn't make out what they were saying. One man was at the stern. He shouted, "The dinghy." The flashlight spun around.

Dan yanked the starter cord. The outboard motor wagged its head back and forth as if in refusal. He yanked the cord again. The little outboard motor shuddered and refused again.

"Dan, they're getting in your dinghy, hurry."

Dan yanked three times quickly. "Paddle," he gasped.

"Paddle?"

"Yes."

What good would paddling do? she wondered.

Furiously, Dan tried to start the intruders' motor. Furiously, the intruders tried to start Dan's motor. Neither cooperated.

Teri paddled.

One of the intruders began to paddle.

Carpe Diem's lights came on. Neville was on the bow saying something.

Dan still tinkered. "Don't worry, they won't get mine started. I have a theft device on it."

He stood up and yanked again and again.

Teri said, "Maybe they have one too."

"No. I think I just flooded it. It'll start in a minute."

The intruders were gaining.

Dan paddled. He said, "Aren't they supposed to yell, 'Stop, police!'"

"Dan, those aren't cops." There were no support boats, no helicopters, no floodlights—just two guys and a rubber dinghy.

"Then who are they?"

"I don't know." She kept paddling though her arms were beginning to tire. "How'd they find us?" Teri whispered.

"I don't know."

"It must have something to do with contacting the lawyer or the private detective. Maybe that was a mistake. I think they connected the dots—they knew your name from the retainer checks."

Dan mumbled as he stood again, "I gave them cash."

"*Cash?*" It seemed like a lot of money to hand over in cash.

"Yeah, I didn't want them to know who—" He pulled. "I—" He yanked. "—was." After a pause, he yanked again. The motor sputtered. He yanked once more and it sputtered and shook like it was going to shake itself down to loose screws and tiny pieces. Then abruptly it caught and roared. Dan eased back the throttle, knocked it into gear, and cranked the throttle out again. The dinghy quickly rose up onto a plane and skimmed across the silky black water out of the lagoon.

Teri wanted to talk, but the wail of the engine made conversation difficult and she didn't want to scream out into the black night. She held on tight to a side rope. It was like flying a carpet, gliding fast and smooth through the cool velvety abyss. Her hair fluttered and whipped the side of her face. They whisked past an unlit green marker. There was no moon. They zipped from one flashing channel marker to the next, hoping they wouldn't ram into one of the unlit poles.

They were fleeing for their lives, yet the cool crisp breeze in her face, the swift smooth ride, the darkness, the lights—the feeling was exhilarating. Here and now it was almost fun. It was a short-lived sensation, but she enjoyed the thrill until she began to wonder again, *How had they found us, and who were they? Who really killed Hill?* It seemed impossible to keep hiding or that she and Dan could prove her innocence. But somehow for the moment they were okay.

The waterway was widening. Lights appeared ahead and rapidly grew in size and number. They were entering Hobe sound. The land on the ocean side was dotted with palm trees, vast rolling lawns and gardens. Elegant waterfront homes were illuminated by flood lights and the boats at their docks were the size of small houses. The mainland side was more modest, crammed with rows of waterfront bungalows.

The outboard motor began to falter.

"Running out of gas," Dan muttered as he turned the dinghy out of the channel. They coasted to a halt near a home with a concrete wharf and a small aluminum fishing boat hauled up out of the water on a steel hoist.

It was quiet once more, and still. Teri picked up where she had left off, whispering, "They must have figured out who you were from the rental van. I think someone watched you leave and got the plate numbers. You must have used a license and a credit card for that?"

Dan grabbed a red plastic jug, and shook it. He unscrewed the lid. "Yeah. I didn't want to but it was the only way."

"Maybe the detective?"

"Maybe a clerk at the law office . . . it doesn't matter who."

With a rumble, a tall sportfisherman emerged from one of the canals and motored slowly into the waterway.

"So they've got your name. They know you're helping me." Teri squeezed his forearm. "I'm sorry. You're really in deep now." *Was that why he had turned cool towards her? Was he regretting his rash decision to help?*

From a plastic milk crate wedged into the stern Dan pulled out a small bottle. "What I can't figure out is, how did they do it all so quickly?"

"Internet?" Teri suggested. "I don't know. They must know what they're doing, must have pretty good access to classified information. From car rental plates, to your name—somebody knows what they're doing."

He poured oil into the red jug.

"From your name, I guess they got the name of your boat."

"I'm a foreigner on a cruising permit," Dan mumbled. "So they keep records on me. And all bridge tenders keep a list of every boat that passes through. They could narrow it down pretty easily."

"But it wasn't the police that found us."

He screwed the lid back on. The dinghy had drifted clear of the channel and had almost reached the concrete wharf.

Teri continued, "It should have been the police. I can almost believe that the cops could be that quick, but that definitely *wasn't* the police. Whoever figured it out didn't tell the police. Maybe they told someone else."

"Maybe it was a network thing, and it just sort of spread."

"That quickly? Amazing." Teri pondered this.

"Or maybe they told the police and a cop leaked it out to someone." He poured the mixed fuel into the tank.

"Why?"

"I have no idea. I think there's a mysterious separate world out there and we outsiders have no idea how it operates."

Dan squeezed the rubber bulb, pumping fuel to the motor. "Seems like they're ganging up on us."

They had drifted close to the concrete wall. "Maybe we can stay here somewhere?" Teri reached out and fended off. Up on the shore there were small bungalows, with white vinyl siding, big windows and screened-in Florida rooms. "Where were you thinking of going?"

Frustrated, Dan sank down to sit on a tube. "That lighthouse?" He pointed in the direction the sportfisherman had been heading. There was a lighthouse, tall and red, like a huge stick of candy. "That's Jupiter Inlet. Tonight is pretty calm . . . if I could get more gas, well, I was trying to figure out if we could make it to the Bahamas."

"In a rubber dinghy? Cross the Gulf Stream? Really?"

"Well, it was one idea. Be an adventure. And if I had more gas, and a recent weather forecast, and a compass . . . A handheld radio would be nice. Drinking water. Charts."

Teri stood up, still holding onto the concrete wall. "What were some of your other ideas?"

"Well." Dan shrugged. "I'm running a little low on ideas at the moment."

She looked over the wharf at the dark house they were in front of. "I've got one."

Dan wondered what she had seen and started to stand, but there was nothing to see. Most of the houses were dark. They looked empty.

Teri found his eyes. She tried to muster up some bravado. "I'll just turn myself in. Maybe I could say I forced you to help me."

Dan chuckled. "Yeah sure. Threatened me."

Another tall sportfisherman rumbled slowly down the waterway towards the inlet. Poking high out of the stern was an array of fishing rods, long as the lances of a medieval knight.

Teri felt a calmness come over her. The idea of turning

herself in would wash away the uncertainty, the anxiety. If nothing else, it might save Dan. She thought about jail, and that thought scared her. She tried not to be scared, but she wasn't ready for jail. She looked at Dan. No, she didn't want to go to jail. She remembered the innocent touch of his feet on hers, and she knew she wasn't ready to say goodbye. That would be harder than jail. It was like there was some unfinished business to attend to and she thought it would be nice to salvage one more day, one more night together. If she was going to jail, she wanted to paste a few more stolen moments in her scrapbook, a few more memories to comfort her in the lonely days looming ahead.

"Well, we can't just stand here." He bent forward and made a stirrup with his hands. Teri stepped in and put her hand on his shoulders and kneeled up onto the wall. He handed her a line. Then he disconnected the fuel tank and hoisted it up.

"What are you doing?"

"I don't want to pollute the water."

Teri took the fuel tank from him and carried it over to the hoist where the fishing boat was and left it there. It didn't look out of place.

Meanwhile Dan unscrewed the valves in the dinghy and the air came whistling out. By the time he hauled himself up onto the concrete wall, the dinghy was already soft and spongy.

"Did you have to do that?" she asked, watching the dinghy collapse in upon itself.

"Better they don't know where we went." He started to walk.

"I thought I was turning myself in."

"Naw."

"No?"

"Look, it's a beautiful morning, just smell that air . . . and it's going to be a spectacular sunrise." While he continued to talk, Teri glanced back over her shoulder. The sun would be rising soon, but right now the sky looked like lead. "You don't want to go to jail today, do you? Besides, we're making good progress here."

"We are?"

"Sure." The dinghy sank into the black water, a stream of bubbles hissed and gurgled.

"We're still alive. We're free."

Teri was beside him. "Right. I don't know if technically you can call that progress—I was alive and free yesterday with only the police chasing me, and the day before that I was alive and free with a job, a future and no one at all chasing me, and—"

"Yes, but . . ."

In front of the house there was a small pool in a large screened-in addition. They rounded the pool and stood at the side wall. The house was quiet and all the drapes were drawn.

Dan whispered, "But now we've learned that somebody other than the police is after you."

A hedge and some thick green shrubs blocked their progress; they had to push their way through. They reached the corner of the house. Their eyes darted across the street and into the shadows. They cut across the lawn.

"And that's progress?"

He took her hand for a moment, to lead her around a

large cabbage palmetto and a small garden with a ceramic elf in the middle.

"Sure."

"Why is that progress?"

There was no car in the driveway. They crossed the lawn. The grass was wet with dew.

"Because, why are they after you?"

"I don't know." *Why would someone go to all the trouble of trying to usurp the responsibility of the law enforcement authorities?* She contemplated that as they skirted the sprawling fronds of a royal palm.

She was glad to reach the road, but immediately regretted being out in the open, exposed. The truth was, she didn't feel comfortable anywhere.

Dan said, "What about the actual murderer? The cops think you killed Hill."

"Yes, I get that feeling."

"But what about the real murderer?"

"Obviously, the real murderer knows I didn't kill anybody."

"Of course, but do they know you saw *them* kill Hill?"

Teri thought about this.

"I mean if you're a witness—"

"The police won't believe me. Surely you don't think the police would believe me?"

"That's not exactly what I'm driving at. What I'm thinking is, if the killer thinks you might have recognized him, might he also be hunting you?"

She considered that. "Perhaps."

"I mean, right now he's sitting pretty. The world is certain you killed Hill. Only two people—three if you include me—know that that isn't true: you and the real murderer. Whether or not you saw him, with you gone . . ."

"They might prefer me dead."

"Yes. I just wanted to get that straight."

"I see. I feel much better now. That certainly is progress all right."

"It's not just the cops after you, the real murderer might like to find you, too. And get rid of you, so you can't talk and prove your innocence and risk implicating him."

"Yes, I think you've made your point."

"Well, it's just something that occurred to me. I wanted to share it with you."

"Thanks." They walked down the middle of the street.

Teri murmured, "So, everyone is after me."

Every few steps there was a mailbox and a concrete driveway. Occasionally newspapers lay strewn on the damp ground wrapped in plastic bags. They both glanced down trying to discern the headlines as they walked by.

"And that's your idea of progress? Now instead of being arrested and getting a fair trial, or at least a reasonably fair trial, I'm going to be killed. That's your idea of making good progress?"

"Sure. Whoever killed Hill is probably behind whoever is trying to get you now."

"Probably?"

"Well, we don't know for sure, but it's possible."

"That is good news. That's great."

"Yeah," he responded with a smirk.

"So maybe we're getting close to the actual murderer?"

"Well, more accurately, I think maybe the actual murderer is getting closer to us. We don't know for sure. It's a crazy world. But I think it's a reasonable guess."

The streets were very quiet, but she could hear the hum of cars in the distance. Even at this early hour, there was a busy street nearby.

"Maybe," Teri started and stopped before saying, "We should have tried to grab them back at the boat instead of running away."

Dan looked at her like she might be crazy. "Yeah right." A car came to a rolling stop at a cross street then carried on.

Teri watched and waited until it was out of sight and said, "Or maybe we should just get away from here. The idea of running far away and hiding out until this all blows over is beginning to sound really appealing."

"We're still within a few miles of Hill's home."

Teri stepped up the pace. "Far away. California. How about Canada?"

"I don't want to go back there right now, too cold. I'll take you in June."

"Promise?"

"Sure. We'll go sailing on Georgian Bay. There are thirty thousand uninhabited islands and the water is so clean you can just drink from the lake. Nobody would find us there."

Teri glanced in the rear window of a big white Cadillac as she walked past. Dan kept talking, "So, how'd you like sailing so far?"

"Seems kind of slow."

"Yeah, it is that." He spoke as though slowness was one of the wonderful attributes.

"First of all we have to get away from here."

* * *

They continued to follow the sound of the traffic, until Teri stopped at the rear of a blue Chevy Cavalier. It was parked on the side of the road. She nodded at the car. "Let's steal this."

Dan looked at her. "The car?" He walked around peering in the windows. The Chevy was a few years old but in good shape—a common, unremarkable car. Probably a good choice if you wanted to steal a car and blend in. "You want to steal this car?" he asked.

Teri nodded.

Dan nodded in response.

"I mean, if it bothers you—stealing a car—maybe we could leave a note," Teri suggested. "Offer to reimburse."

"Extenuating circumstances."

"Right. Maybe the owner would understand."

"Sure. I could buy the car. Give them twice what it's worth, just to be safe."

Teri added quickly, "And I could pay you back."

"There we go. It's all settled." He was still looking inside. It was clean and tidy with a nylon wind breaker on the passenger seat and a cardboard Garfield sunshade folded up on the back ledge.

"Okay Dan?"

"Sure, if you say so."

Neither of them touched the car.

Impatiently Teri asked, "What's the matter? You don't like the idea?"

"No, it's an okay idea."

"So what are you waiting for?"

"Me?" He shrugged. "Well, I don't have a pen, do you have a pen?"

"We don't have to write the note right now. I mean we can probably find out whose it is, write an apology and mail it with a check."

Dan nodded.

"But we shouldn't just hang around here, looking like we're thinking about stealing the car." There were lights on in some of the houses. They'd seen one person come out in slippers and a bathrobe to retrieve their morning paper.

"Right."

"Somebody might see us." Teri looked at Dan. "So we should hurry." She looked at the closest house; it was dark and quiet. She looked back at Dan. "What?" she asked.

"Okay, do it," he said.

Teri hesitated. Her eyes narrowed. "Me?"

Dan nodded.

"Me?" Teri repeated, feeling a little confused.

"It was your idea."

"So what if it was my idea? I don't know how to steal a car. What kind of a woman do you think I am? *I* don't know how to steal a car. You steal it."

"What? You just assume I know how to steal a car? I don't know how to steal a car."

Teri's hands flew up and spread wide apart. "You just hot-wire it."

"Hot-wire what?"

"The ignition. Some wires—"

"What wires?" He tried the door handle. "How do I get inside? The door is locked."

"Of course it's locked." He looked the type that could hot-wire a car. "Haven't you ever gotten into a locked car?"

"Sure, I call the auto club, but this time—"

"That's great." She turned around in a huff and started walking away.

"Maybe if I had a coat hanger." When he looked up he noticed she was leaving, stalking down the street. "Just a second, you're mad at me because I don't know how to steal a car?"

Chapter Five

More cars drove by. More people came out to grab their newspapers. It was that time of morning when everyone was stirring, busy.

"Hungry?"

Teri hadn't been until he mentioned it, but now she was ravenous. She nodded, then said, "You know, I'm sorry about the car thing." She'd thought about it and he was right, assuming someone was capable of car theft . . . that was terrible.

"My fault." Dan countered. "I hung around with the wrong crowd. Should have misspent more of my youth. Never even been to jail. Yet."

Teri ignored his sarcasm and scowled, but the scowl quickly withered and she tried to explain. "I just so wanted to get into that car and zip away, 'cause this . . ."

"Is the pits?" Dan suggested.

"Yes. It is. I feel so vulnerable walking out in the open."

"I know what you mean," he said, his voice calm and even. "The same friendly people we keep saying good morning to are about to open their papers and see pictures and stories about you." They exchanged a glance.

Teri felt her blood beginning to percolate, her anxiety building. "We need a car or something. We need to get out of here."

"Don't know how we can get a car. Can't steal one. Can't rent one."

Rounding one more street corner Teri could see the back walls of small stores. They were near a main road. Her pace slackened. "So, what are we doing? Where are we going?" She felt panic stretching through her. She was confronted with the shimmering ebb and flow of endless traffic—more and more people, people everywhere. She didn't have a clue what to do. At college there hadn't been courses like, *How to Prove You're Not a Murderer 101*. She'd never come across a book titled *The Dummies Guide to Being a Fugitive*.

"We've got to have some sort of plan."

"We should." Dan shrugged.

They cut across the back of a parking lot. As they approached, a clutch of seagulls scattered.

"Maybe I could phone an old buddy."

"Who?" she asked.

"I don't think you know him."

"Of course I don't know him."

"Well, you might."

Until they rounded the corner and caught sight of the

sign, they didn't realize they were behind a convenience store.

"I might?"

"Do you read the sports pages?"

"No."

"Then I guess you won't."

They stepped up onto the curb. A small gray Toyota was parked close to the front door. Teri shied away from the faces in the cars waiting at the traffic lights. She looked at her bare feet and realized her soles hurt. She looked at the candy wrappers stuck flat on the sun bleached asphalt. Then she looked up at the wide hood of a car rolling into the lot, a big car with printing on the fenders: a police car. It surged up the slight rise to the curb and stopped. Two policemen were clearly visible through the front windshield.

She was ready to run, but her knees seized and it was all she could do to walk without toppling over. A phone booth offered minimal privacy, but she leaned in and picked up the receiver. Her limbs were trembling.

The car doors groaned as they opened.

Close beside her Dan reached down and snared the empty blue plastic cover. "Never any phone books in Florida." He let the shell drop on its chain. "Do people steal phone books?"

The car doors slammed, one after the other. The engine was still running. Teri twisted around and stole a glimpse at the two policemen standing beside the car. They were talking. They were in uniform. They were both young and tall with crew cuts. One was working on a mustache. They were looking at her. With great effort she managed not to crumble.

An hour ago she had decided to turn herself in—so what if the cops arrested her? She would have preferred to have the dignity of turning herself in, but either way she'd just let herself be arrested and go to jail. The thought of jail caused her to stop breathing—she was terrified of jail. And once in jail she might not ever get out again.

"Are you going to use the phone?" Dan asked. He took it from her trembling hand, and replaced it with a kiss to the palm. That caught her by surprise and she snapped her hand away. Dan mumbled, "You know, I'm not pleased about this turn of events either." He checked for change in the coin return. "But so far so good."

"Something's good? What's good?" The words crawled out between her teeth. "You're always saying things are good. Nothing—"

"Relax," he whispered. "Please." His eyes slid slowly over her face. He smiled as if to apologize for the situation. His easy smile was annoying; paradoxically, it was also calming. Dan dropped a coin into the phone. She heard the coin tinkle along its route.

"Haven't pulled," he murmured in a barely audible whisper, "their guns. Don't," he keyed in the first number, "seem excited. We're just making a phone call." He finished dialing. "Nothing special."

Teri tried not to look, but she could see them. "They're coming towards us! Why don't we just calmly wander away." In her mind her feet were already scampering. "Across the street to Burger King." She spoke as low and as slow as she could manage, "You're hungry, remember?"

"I'm starving," he agreed with a casual nod.

In a daze she heard Dan ask for the phone number of

someone named Trevor Symes. He waited and said to her, "Remember two, two, oh, seven."

Teri turned and risked another glance back. The policemen were next to them, she could have reached out and touched them, but they didn't stop. They passed and opened the doors of the convenience store.

Dan repeated, "Two, two, oh, seven."

Teri repeated, "Two, two, oh, seven." The policemen were gone. The glass doors eased closed behind them.

Dan hung up the phone and said, "You don't have change, right? I need more change."

She waited until the store doors were completely closed then whispered, "Let's get out of here."

"Watch the bags for a sec." He left the phone booth. "Want anything?"

She started to follow him, but he went into the store. In stunned disbelief she watched him follow the policemen into the store. She looked across the street at the Burger King. She forced herself to think, *Keep cool, casual, nonchalant.* Then Teri picked up the phone. She had no one to call. Her mother had died three years ago. Her father was in a nursing home, his mind erased by Alzheimer's. Her mind was a pinball machine; random thoughts were ricocheting off the walls. Here she was moments away from life in prison and she was wondering why she didn't have a close friend she could call up and chat with. "Yes, they think I killed him, can you imagine? Such a silly mistake." Teri held the phone ready.

The plate glass door opened and a young woman in nurse whites came out. Teri turned her back and pretended to chat into the phone. The woman sunk into the Toyota. She backed up the car and drove away.

Then the door opened again and Dan emerged with a small bag. He had newspapers tucked under his arm. He wore cheap rubber sandals and handed her a pair. "Guess what? They're here looking for that woman, the one who murdered that guy, Hill." He handed her the newspapers. "Here, why don't you check on what's new in the world?"

Teri grimaced. She snatched the papers.

Dan continued to speak as he bent over, put the bags on the concrete and began to search through them. "They're talking to the clerks. Telling them to keep an eye peeled for her—you know, armed and dangerous, don't try to apprehend, just report any sightings." He handed Teri a small carton.

She screamed, "Milk?"

"You don't like milk? It's good for you." He took the milk back, and checked in his bag. "Orange juice? Apple juice? Iced tea, regular or raspberry? I can run back in and get you a coffee, but that's where—"

Teri grabbed the orange juice from him.

Dan picked up the phone. "They showed me a picture." He started to drop in coins all the while making a point of scrutinizing her face. "You know, I can see the resemblance, but in that picture you're all dolled up, and well, now, after your swim and all—"

"I look like a rat?"

"No! You just look—"

"Like a drowned rat."

"No you look good, you just look more casual, more real than this babe here." He nodded to the picture in the newspaper as he punched in several numbers. "She's posing for a magazine cover." He kept admiring the photo. "What was that number?" With his teeth he ripped open a cellophane pack of two chocolate caramel cakes. He offered her one.

Teri shook her head. She was still looking at the newspaper picture. "And what? This me," Teri pointed at herself with a thumb, "I'm posing for a mug shot? Oh, what difference does it make!" She remembered the day the picture was taken. She knew graduation photos could follow people through life and she did 'doll' herself up.

He took a bite from a cake, then he split open the little carton of milk and took a swig. Dan looked away and mumbled loudly enough for her to hear, "Why are the pretty ones always so sensitive about their looks?" He shook his head adding, just as the police emerged from the store, "As if you've got something to worry about." He took another swig of milk.

Again Dan asked her for the number but Teri stared at the phone. The cops glanced over. Dan made eye contact and nodded as if to say, 'Hi guys, you know me, you saw me in the store already.' He kept the phone to his ear. "That number I asked you to remember?" He took another bite.

Teri whispered, "Dan, let's get out of here."

"Just a second. Was it two, two, oh, seven?"

"Sure. Whatever."

"Thanks." He finished dialing. He kept looking at the newspaper then he said, "Nice picture though. Hair color looks different." Dan turned the phone so Teri could hear. It was ringing.

The police approached. Her mouth suddenly felt like cotton. She couldn't stop herself from staring directly at them. Her spine hummed.

Dan whispered, "You dye your hair?"

The two policemen were close.

It took her a moment to digest what Dan had said. She looked away from the cops and stared at Dan in disbelief. She thumped him in the arm.

Dan feigned embarrassment. "Sorry, that was rude. Nice color though."

The two policemen headed to their car. They each carried jumbo coffee cups.

Teri said excitedly under her breath, "They're leaving."

"Probably just calling for backup—SWAT team, helicopters. We're far too dangerous for two mere patrolmen to handle all on their own."

"I don't think you should joke about this."

"I have to."

"Why?"

"Because, I'm as scared as you are. And that's how I deal with stress."

"Really?"

"Yes, I think so."

"Does it work?"

The policemen slid into their car.

"So far," Dan said. He offered her the remaining cake. Teri was tempted. She looked at the cake. She was very tempted, but the cake didn't go with orange juice. She looked at his milk; now the milk looked appealing. Tightlipped, she shook her head.

"I thought you had a sweet tooth?"

She shook her head again.

"You're sure?" he asked.

"Yes! I'm sure."

Dan shrugged. He bit into the chocolate coating.

The phone stopped ringing and a machine answered. Dan hung up and started to dial again. "Two, two, oh, seven, right?"

Teri didn't respond, but Dan kept mumbling away, "Those cops are too busy doing their job to notice you." He washed down the second cake with another gulp of milk. The police car was backing up, it swung across the front of the store to avoid the highway, crossing the small side street into the Burger King lot.

"They don't expect to find you goofing around outside a convenience store making a phone call. They expect you to be skulking somewhere, like in a hotel room, or hopping a freight train, or stealing a car or shooting at somebody. At the very least scurrying away at their approach."

The phone was still ringing.

"You know, it's funny." Dan rambled on, "The boss tells them to drive around showing people the picture, so they do, but they never expect to actually bump into you."

"I get your point. But it scared me half to death."

Dan snickered. "Me too." He finished the milk and crumpled the container. "I was really afraid you might turn yourself in." He shot the carton at a distant garbage bin. It hit the rim and bounced in.

"I probably should have." Teri looked to the traffic. She kept expecting someone to lean out of a car window and point and scream, 'There she is, there she is. Get her!'

He said calmly, "Still can if you want."

"Should I?" Teri asked.

Dan started to shrug. "I can't answer that. That's a biggie. That one has to be all your decision."

There was anxiety in her eyes as she pleaded, "But what do *you* think I should do?"

He finished his shrug. "I can't tell you what to do. You have to make up your own mind. But whatever you decide, I'll help you."

Teri tried to think, tried to decide. Then she said, "I am really not eager to go to jail."

Dan smiled. "Well then, somehow, we just have to sneak away from here."

Teri nodded. Sneak away to where? Deciding it was best not to stare at the traffic, she focused her attention on the papers.

A click from the phone and the ringing stopped.

"Trevor?" Dan asked, his voice rising.

At the other end of the line there was a cough, a moan. The words were slurred. "Yes. Hello."

"Trev, it's me Dan. Dan Parent."

"Dan? Daniel? What . . . time is it?"

"It's early."

After a long silence, Trevor Symes muttered, "So Daniel, what . . . what's the occasion? You're in town?"

"Sort of. There's some big doings."

Teri looked up from the paper. She couldn't get over the extraordinary experience of reading stories about herself. She found herself skimming the articles and developing real disdain for the central character, the murderer. Then she remembered the murderer was her, and the realization felt like someone had cut her knees out from under her.

"Indeed?" Trevor spoke slowly, interrupted with assorted

snorts and sniffles. "A triumphant return to the mighty Maple Leafs. Playoffs looming, eh? Marvelous."

"No, it's bigger than that."

"Bigger?"

"It's about Teri Peterson."

"Who's he?"

"She."

"She?"

"The one accused of murdering T J Hill."

"Daniel, what are you talking about?"

"Don't you read the papers?"

Teri could hear him yawning as he spoke. "You know, just the sports, the Sunday literary supplement."

The front section she was reading got stuffed under her elbow. She switched to the front page of *USA Today*: another picture of her. She noted what Dan mentioned about her being all dolled up. The papers all featured the same college graduation picture, the one she saw in the hands of the police.

"Look, she didn't kill anybody."

"That's splendid, Daniel. But why share this tidbit with me?"

"I thought I'd do you a favor."

"Well, I'm truly honored. Thank you."

Teri was scanning the article. Dan was reading too.

Trevor said, "I surmise you require a reporter for some purpose, but remember Daniel I'm strictly sports page. I can run around informing everyone I meet that I don't believe your lady-friend, and I assume that's what this is about. Daniel, nobody gives a hoot what I think."

"Tomorrow's front page will probably be about me too."

"Really? Be forewarned Daniel—unless it has to do with hockey, nobody cares what you think either."

"Trevor, you could be the first reporter in the world to have the true story of how Hill died. You'll be famous, get a raise. When you walk into a bar all the babes will point and whisper, 'There's—' "

"But Daniel, they do that now." He laughed.

"We'll give you an exclusive."

"We?"

"Yes."

"An exclusive what?"

Dan put his hand over the mouthpiece. "They don't mention your letter."

"They do in this other one," she whispered, "at the end." Teri flipped to another paper.

Trevor moaned again. "I'm still a little sleepy here, you know the hours I keep."

"Trev, look, you can have a direct line to her story, to her, we'll set up an interview. You've always talked about writing a book. You can do lunch with the woman the entire nation is searching for. You can tell her side of the story."

"Here." Teri pointed at a paragraph. The newspaper acknowledged receiving a fax proclaiming her innocence but the police doubted the fax's authenticity. Her version of the murder was not a big deal for the paper.

"Why, Daniel? What is it you want from me?"

"We need someone to say, 'Hold on, maybe she didn't do it.' You can be the first. I don't know how the paper business works but if you write a scoop and it's picked up by other papers around the world, won't you become famous, or rich, or both? What happened to those Watergate guys?"

"That was big stuff."

"*This* is big stuff. I wish it wasn't but it is. They think she killed T J Hill."

Teri stopped reading. She waited for his reaction. It took a while.

"Daniel, are you quite certain she didn't? I've misled you a tad. Actually, I am somewhat acquainted with the incident. At the moment you can't avoid it, it's all anyone speaks of. The evidence seems overwhelming, her guilt seems to be a lock."

"Trev, if you met her and talked to her, you would know she couldn't possibly have killed anyone."

Teri could hear skepticism in the prolonged silence.

"Ah, I see," Trevor answered finally. Then there was another pause. "Exactly what do you want me to do?"

"You can start by saying that ex-hockey player Dan Parent is with Teri and convinced of her innocence."

"Okay, but people will promptly conclude you've been conked in the head with too many hockey pucks."

"That's for tomorrow's paper. Mention that you think we're in the Bahamas. Crossed last night in a rubber dinghy."

"Rubber dinghy? Now, that is marvelous."

"Well, that's just a rumor you've heard. But the letter we faxed to the papers is real. I've got your newspaper here and they think it's a prank, but it's in Teri's handwriting—get someone to check it. And it's true, every word."

"Daniel, they have an eyewitness."

"Can you convict someone on the say-so of one witness?"

"Yes, I'm quite certain they can, indeed. Mind you, they also have fingerprints, the murder weapon, and everything else you can possibly think of. Absolutely convincing."

"Dig into all that. What did the witness actually see? Teri admits she was there, but came in after someone else stabbed him. What was her motive? She had no reason to kill him."

"Motive? That's only germane to an Agatha Christie plot. In the real world an eyewitness and every possible form of physical evidence known to mankind results in conviction, every time, whether she had a reason to murder the poor fellow or not. Who really cares what crackpot reason she might have had?"

Undeterred Dan carried on. "And if she didn't kill him, who did? Who had a reason to kill him?"

"She fled the scene. Innocent people do not flee the scene of a crime and go into hiding."

"You're the writer here Trev, you'll figure out how to handle it."

"Daniel, perhaps you've forgotten, I'm a sports reporter! The moment they find a Yank who is willing to work for my pitiful stipend and is moderately aware of the difference between a hockey puck and a hat trick, I'm toast here. They don't assign me to cover baseball matches or bowling games, just hockey, that's all I'm allotted."

"All the more reason to do this, Trevor. It'll make your name. You'll be big."

Trevor scoffed.

"Front page," Dan added. "Trevor Symes."

Again Trevor was silent.

Dan carried on, enunciating slowly. "Bahamas, rubber dinghy, last night. No motive. She didn't do it. Who might have?"

After a while Trevor said, with resignation, "Yes. I suppose you are accurate in one respect, I have precious little to lose here."

"So you'll meet us?"

"Okay, but I can't promise anything."

"That's okay, I understand. Thanks, and, ah, Trev, is there any way you can bring the paper's what do you call it, archive? The paper's file on Hill?"

"Yes, that shouldn't pose any difficulty. I can do that."

"And, um, Trev, can I borrow a car?"

"A car?"

"Yes. Preferably a van."

"A van?"

"Just a little one. Maybe a camper."

"My camper!" There was a long pause, then Trevor announced, "This sounds an awful lot like aiding and abetting a fugitive."

"Remember she's innocent. You're going to be a hero."

"Marvelous. Heroes. Always fancied being a bit of a hero. Perhaps we heroes can share a cell. Do you play cribbage?"

They discussed a place to meet and Dan finished by saying, "I owe you big time."

Trevor responded, "Yes, indeed," and hung up. Dan looked at Teri. "Anybody you want to call? I've got some change left."

She shook her head and he replaced the receiver. They

picked up their bags and edged out of the phone booth. The traffic flowed by in waves.

Teri muttered, "We have to find a place to hide. We'll stick out like a sore thumb walking in Florida."

She looked at Dan, and he shrugged.

Chapter Six

Side by side they sat on a bench with their backs to the traffic.

"Okay, so Maple Leafs. That's hockey, isn't it? You're a hockey player?"

"Yes, sort of."

"Sort of?"

"I used to be a goalie."

He wasn't speaking loudly. She leaned forward, looked at him and checked to make sure she heard correctly. "A goalie? A hockey goalie?"

"Yes."

Teri leaned back and took another lick of her ice cream cone. Then she repeated, "A hockey goalie?"

"Yes," Dan answered again as though that was more than enough explanation.

"Goalie," she mused. "College correspondence. Unopened textbooks. Sailboat. Florida. Canadian. Dan, I can't figure it all out."

Dan responded with a chuckle before adding, "Me neither." He changed the subject. "Nanny? Mary Poppins fixation?"

"Hardly. I told you before I just needed a job for a year, to make some money and go back to school."

"And the goal?"

"Finish my Ph.D. in early childhood education." She thought if she told him about her situation, he would be compelled to divulge more about himself.

"Ph.D." Dan was impressed—she could hear it in his voice.

They were sitting in a courtyard facing a strip mall and a small fountain, not far from the street corner where they had arranged to meet Trevor.

"Seems a bit of a fantasy now. But I was going to become a teacher, then I wanted to work my way up to school principal, and then, someday," she stopped and exhaled like she was tired just thinking about it. "I had hoped to get involved at the state level directing education policy, maybe even the national level."

"That's great."

"Nothing is more important than education and yet it always seems to lag behind. Teaching hasn't changed much in a hundred years, yet there is so much more to learn, so much more pressure on children. Technology provides fabulous opportunities: long distance communication, research, individual instruction. If an eight-year-old is interested in space, say, you can create a special learning package for him or her, and the Internet can link together like-minded kids from all over the country. Kids have to be challenged and, and . . . I'm boring you."

"No, not at all."

She didn't know whether to continue or not. It certainly seemed to be off topic. Until two days ago her plans had been real, now all hope had evaporated.

"I think it's terrific that you have such a clear idea of your goals."

Teri frowned. Lot of good it would do her in jail.

"You've got it all planned," he said.

She did have it all planned, once.

"I'm envious. I never really planned anything in my life."

"You must have, to become a hockey player."

"No. It just sort of happened."

She scoffed. "Come on."

"Where I was a kid everyone played hockey. I never even thought about it. My dad signed me up, bought the equipment. One Saturday morning he told me to turn off the cartoons, go out and get in the truck, and he drove me to the rink. I sat on the bench and he kneeled down and laced up my skates, handed me a stick, escorted me to the gate and aimed me out onto the ice. It was never discussed. I remember it very clearly. He watched every minute of every game and every practice."

"Where was that?"

"Kirkland Lake. You've never heard of it."

Teri shook her head.

"A mining town in Northern Ontario."

She nodded. Dan asked, "Have you got your entire life mapped out? Everything? How many kids?"

Teri thought she detected mocking in his voice. She didn't answer. Two kids: she could see them in her imagination; blonde, blue eyes, pudgy cheeks, chubby knees . . . though not as clearly as she once did.

Dan suggested, "And you've probably decided on their names."

Rachel and Tommy. It was a reflex, she knew he was teasing.

"And your house."

It would be somewhere in the suburbs: Cape Cod style, big trees, fenced backyard with a really cute matching doghouse.

"What does your husband do?"

For some reason, in her daydreams he was always something like an accountant, she didn't know why. He just went to an office somewhere, jacket and tie, nine to five. But she couldn't think about it much now, her dreams were gone. It didn't require Dan's teasing to drive that home. Nothing would ever be the same. She was tempted to mourn and curse her fate but she didn't think she had the emotional energy to do it. She let the thought slip away. Instead she looked for a cutting remark to fire back at him; he was making fun of her and that made her angry. She hadn't said anything, still she felt like she had told him too much, trusted him.

Then he added, "I'm envious," and he said it in such a sincere and gentle way that she had to believe him.

"What? You don't have dreams?" When he didn't answer, she blundered on, "Wife, kids, home?"

"I have dreams. But they change so often I don't think much about them."

Teri laughed. "Tell me about it." When he just nodded in response she said, "You're injured, right?"

"Yes."

"The knees, right?"

"And left," Dan quipped.

"You seem okay."

"You sound like the Toronto media."

"What's that mean?"

"Nothing."

"And you thought you'd take some correspondence courses while you recuperated."

"That's about it."

"Preparing for life after hockey. That's good."

"Seemed like a good idea at the time."

"So what's the problem?"

"No problem. Everything is going exactly according to plan."

"That's great," she mocked him. "Me too, pretty much." A moment later she added somberly, "I think we're kidding ourselves, aren't we?"

"About what?"

"About figuring a way out of this mess, about figuring out who really killed Hill. We don't know what we're doing. Even if we miraculously discover who murdered him, we still have to prove it. How could we do that?" She tossed the end of her cone into a garbage can. "They're going to catch us eventually."

"Perhaps. Yes, I guess it's inevitable."

"So what are we doing?"

"I don't know, putting up a fight? Trying our best to figure out who really killed him? It's not completely hopeless. Maybe sometimes things in life are hopeless, but this isn't hopeless."

"It's almost hopeless."

He agreed. "It's a challenge. You seem undaunted by the prospect of getting a Ph.D. and becoming a national policy maker, but to me that sounds far more intimidating than figuring out who killed Hill."

"It's not. You just have to set your mind to it, then work hard. Figuring out who killed Mr. Hill, that's different," Teri said. "I know I can work hard, I want to work hard. Hard work has never been a problem for me. But trying to figure out who killed Mr. Hill, what do I work at? Where do I begin? How do I go about this? I can't even risk going to a library to do research about him. Where do I focus my energy? Maybe that file from your friend will help." That was something she could do. She didn't want to let her hopes get too high. What sort of clues could be in a newspaper file?

Dan continued, "Well, you're obviously a very organized person, the unknown must be hard for you. I'm not all that organized. I'm sort of accustomed to winging it like this."

An older couple in matching sweat suits came out of 'Strictly Pâté' carrying a small package. It was a quiet plaza, with an odd mix of stores. 'Barstools To Go,' 'Shot Glass Heaven.'

Dan said, "Maybe we already know things that we don't even know we know."

"Pardon?"

"Well . . ." A new thought came from nowhere. "What about the knife?"

"What about it?"

Dan pondered. "What kind of a knife was it?"

Teri tried to remember. "Just a plain knife, I think."

"But why a knife? Aren't there easier ways? Was it a switchblade? Anything fancy?"

"No. It was just a knife, like a regular kitchen knife."

"Steak knife?"

Teri thought about that. She tried to remember. "Sort of, I guess. Bigger maybe."

"Was there a dinner tray in the room?"

"I don't know. I know he sometimes ate at his desk."

Dan nodded, thoughtful. "Why would anyone use a kitchen knife?" he asked. "What a crazy way to kill some-one. Would you use a kitchen knife?"

"I don't know. I'm not a murderer."

"But still."

"If I was in a hurry I might. If that's all there was." She realized what he was driving at: most likely the murder wasn't planned, it was impulsive. The murderer was in a hurry. She considered that. Still it didn't point to anyone. So what if the murder was a sudden impulse, that didn't prove who the murderer was. They sat in the sun thinking.

"Dan, in case something happens all of a sudden, I want to thank you."

"Nothing is going to happen all of a sudden."

"I want you to know how much I appreciate all you have done for me, even the teasing. I know you do it just to distract me, to keep my spirits up."

"I do?"

"Yes, you do." She turned to face him. "Don't you?"

"Oh, sure. 'Course I do."

She stared into his eyes. "I just want to thank you. You understand?"

Dan nodded slow. "Yes, I think I understand. You want to thank me."

Teri looked away and found herself staring into the curious face of a small gray lizard.

"Does this," Dan asked, "mean you won't be sending me that card?"

Motionless, the lizard stared back. She remembered the promised card from the first night. "Is that what you really want, Dan? A card?"

Dan paused like he was carefully weighing his options. "A card would be nice."

A card, Teri thought. "Okay, I'll send you a card first chance I get."

"That'll be great."

The lizard wasn't going to move. She reached out slowly. His eyes blinked, but he didn't move until the last possible second, then he darted away so fast she didn't even know which direction he had gone.

Teri closed her eyes. "I bet," she mumbled, "I bet you wish you had never even met me. Look what I've done to you. You should be in the Bahamas by now, with your friends."

"I may wish a lot of things, you know, but that's not one of them."

"You *should* wish you never met me."

"That's true. I really should."

Teri nodded.

Then Dan added, "But, you know, it just doesn't work that way."

A few moments later, he said, "Remember, you did nothing wrong. The very idea of you attacking Hill with a knife . . ."

"Who could?" She shook her head in bewilderment. *Who could kill someone with a knife like that?* "It had to be someone in the house, didn't it?"

"Wasn't someone off the street. I wouldn't think you'd plan a murder by hoping to find a weapon on the premises."

"No. Someone in the house."

"Spur of the moment. Grabbed the first weapon they saw."

"So something had to provide the impetus," Teri said. "It wasn't a planned assassination. It wasn't planned at all. You don't work out a plan to kill someone and base it on finding a weapon at the scene."

Dan asked, "Anything sudden or unexpected happen at the house?"

Teri couldn't think of anything but mumbled, "Now that I think about it Mr. Hill usually visited the kids at bedtime and that night he didn't." She looked over at Dan. Was that significant? What could that mean? "Maybe something important was going on, but I wouldn't know. I feel terrible for those kids. They did have a nice father. It must be horrible for them and for Karen."

Ironically, as a fugitive on the lam it was the waiting that was the most excruciating part, the constant inaction. You felt like you should be doing something, but there didn't seem to be anything to do. The running was easy; waiting calmly was tough. A part of her again began to consider the benefits of succumbing to a nervous collapse.

"So," Dan began, "probably somebody in the house. We started with billions of suspects, and now we're down to a few, and you don't think we're making progress? Hedoby is supposed to be working on a list of everyone in the house."

Teri considered that. It was progress, but somehow it seemed like getting to the moon by climbing the tallest tree. "Hedoby might have been the one to blab about you and the rental van."

"Maybe. We'll see."

After a time, Teri suggested, "What if we call Grant and Hedoby and set up another meeting? It will probably leak again, like it did before, then we grab them and find out who they are or who they work for."

"Okay, that's a great idea." Dan answered without enthusiasm. "How do we do it?" he asked.

"What?"

"Capture two thugs who are probably armed and experienced felons."

"I don't know. But you're a tough guy, a hockey player."

Dan laughed. "I was a goalie."

"So?"

"Goalies aren't tough. Goalies don't fight. We don't get involved in any of that stuff. That's the other players. Sorry."

Teri gave that serious consideration before saying, "We can set a trap."

"Okay," Dan responded. A moment later he asked, "What kind of trap?"

"I don't know."

"Me neither. I guess we'll have to work out the fine points of our plan."

Teri hopped into the front passenger seat. Dan shut the back door. Trevor grinned and pressed the gas pedal.

Trevor Symes was wearing a linen suit in a vanilla shade with a crisp white shirt, white shoes and a pale peach colored tie. He looked like Florida's version of a leprechaun: short, tanned, hair moussed. He spoke with unbridled giddiness, "Where to, my desperadoes?"

Dan shrugged.

"No plans?"

Dan said, "We want to find out who the real murderer is."

"Splendid. How?"

Dan didn't hesitate, "Digging, plugging. We don't know how, exactly." He went on to explain what they did know, about the lawyer and the private investigator, the knife and the house and the people in it. Trevor nodded with a sincerity that seemed feigned. "So for the moment you need to disappear?"

Dan nodded. "We need a place where we can relax a bit and try to figure out what's going on."

"Well, worry not, for I have given your predicament careful contemplation." In an excited voice he explained that he had made a few arrangements. "Unless you prefer an alternative strategy?"

"No." Dan glanced up to Teri. She responded with a shake of her head.

He was driving away from the ocean. Already the congestion of the coast was diminishing.

"Well, there's plenty of food on board." He glanced over to Teri. "My dear, grab that satchel underneath your seat."

Teri reached down and drew out a canvas bag. She handed it to Dan, who moved forward to squat on one knee on the floor between the front seats. He unzipped the bag. On top there was a thick envelope. He took it out and folded back the flap.

"A little pocket money. Always handy," Trevor said.

Dan approximated the middle and handed half the bills up to Teri. "My agent will reimburse you," he said to Trevor.

"Indeed he will."

Teri looked at the stack of cash, unsure of what she was supposed to do with it. Dan stuffed his half in his pockets, then he reached into the bag again. "A cell phone." He held it up and added, "Feels just like Christmas."

"And an American passport," Trevor nodded towards the satchel.

Dan pulled out the small blue book. "Trevor, I'm impressed."

"And those pages in the bottom, that's everything our researchers have on your Mr. Hill."

That's what Teri was after. She divided the cash into four smaller bundles and put a wad into each pocket of her shorts. Then she picked up a few of the pages and began to look through them while Dan flipped the passport open.

"Trev, this guy doesn't look anything like me. Look at the long blonde hair. Five foot eight!" He examined it closer. "It expired in nineteen seventy seven."

"Best I could do. Just don't let anyone open it and you'll be okay."

"Don't let—"

"Flash it with authority."

"So, how'd you get this guy's passport?"

"Had it for years."

Trevor was a story teller. As the Volkswagen waddled onto the Beeline Highway, he gleefully launched into a long tale about when he was a young lad whose one and only objective was to "imbibe prodigious quantities of Mezcal" and lay naked on the beach in Baja California, Mexico—he pronounced it *Bah-ha Calee-forn-yah, Meh-hee-ko*. On one of his forays back into the States to restock the van with "spam and canned peaches," he picked up a hitchhiker. In the customs lineup at the border, the hitchhiker decided to get out and stretch his legs. Thereupon the fellow vanished.

"I was young and foolish. I failed to comprehend the situation, although I had a hunch something was amiss. On the Yank side of the border, I noticed the chap once more. He stood on the shoulder of the road, smirking and anticipating my arrival. I gave him a jaunty wave and carried on my way.

"Some weeks later I was changing a flat and found a burlap sack taped into the undercarriage. I was already back in Mexico at the time, which I considered a tad ironic."

"Drugs?"

"No, little silver trinkets. Jewelry. I think he was one of those chaps who sets up a table on the sidewalk to hawk his wares. Very popular in the seventies. The fellow was smuggling Mexican silver across the border."

"And the passport?"

"I discovered it sitting on the passenger seat. I don't

know if he forgot it, or if it was somehow part of his scheme. I suspect he used his driver's license as identification and the passport was some sort of a back-up plan. His address was in San Diego, perhaps he thought the passport would incline me to pick him up, or if we missed at the border, I would drop it by his home where he could recover his booty."

"I probably should have picked him up and asked him, but I was a trifle miffed at the time. I didn't know about the cache, but quite frankly he was the snooty type and I didn't much fancy his company." Trevor laughed, he almost cackled when he laughed. Dan laughed along with him.

Teri failed to see much humor. She was still stymied by the image of a naked, inebriated Trevor prowling a beach in *Meh-hee-ko*. It almost prevented her from being able to read through the sheets. Most of what she read she already knew.

They had ventured beyond the suburbs, the strip malls and golf courses. The horizon moved back, greened and flattened.

"You know, until the police broke the story late last evening of your involvement with Miss Peterson, the newsroom gods were quite obstinate—they viewed me like I had gone quite loopy. Now, they hang upon my every utterance. When I informed them of my luncheon with you today, they went absolutely gaga."

"You told them?" Dan and Teri both said as they quickly checked the highway behind. Not a car in sight.

Trevor said, "Not to worry. No one back there. I made sure of that before our rendezvous."

Shifting down Trevor signaled and turned off the Bee-line. The road became narrower and more barren, cutting straight through flat green fields. "I had to tell them so they'd hold the front page for me." He checked his watch. "I have to file by nine. Oodles of time yet." A moment later he pulled off the road and rolled to a stop at a picnic table in a park by the side of Lake Okeechobee.

Teri continued to read. She'd barely scratched the surface of her stack of notes.

Trevor turned to Teri. "So, my dear, let's start at the beginning, shall we? Tell me your story. Don't leave anything out." He produced a small tape recorder, which he put up on the dash.

Reluctantly Teri put away her notes. She attempted to begin with the night of the murder but Trevor insisted she "Start with birth!"

"My birth?"

"Yes, of course. When you were born, where you were born. The entire enchilada. Don't leave out a single incident."

Chapter Seven

Relating the story of her life had been hard enough, but reliving the night of the murder had been agony. Again she suffered the horror of watching a good man die a grisly death while in her arms. She finished, then exhaled slowly and closed her eyes. She could feel the eyes of Dan and Trevor upon her.

"Thank you my dear," Trevor said. "I cannot even imagine how difficult this has been for you."

Teri swallowed.

Picking up his tape recorder Trevor turned it off and slipped it into his pocket.

She took the glass Dan had given her, brought the rim to her lips, but abruptly stopped. "Trevor, the only reason I ran was because someone was shooting at me. I didn't want to run. I didn't run at all initially, but when someone is shooting at you . . . I was scared, I shouldn't have run. I panicked. Then it just seemed like no one was going to believe me. Once you start running it's hard to stop. Now I'm afraid. I saw the person who murdered Mr. Hill, and I think they're after me. Somehow they found us before the police."

"Yes, I understand."

"I shouldn't have run."

"At such a moment, who knows . . ." Trevor stopped as Teri interjected, "If I hadn't run at least I wouldn't have dragged Dan into this mess."

"This my dear, is life. Spontaneous. Real. No second chances and no rewind buttons I'm afraid."

While Teri was relating her life story Dan had prepared a meal. As he passed the plates he said, "We think it was one of the people in the house. They heard something, quite possibly from Hill himself, and got angry—"

Trevor nodded. "Angry indeed."

"Yes, and grabbed whatever weapon was readily at hand, and killed him. That should be in your story."

They took their plates out of the little Volkswagen and sat at the picnic table.

Trevor glanced over at Teri. He looked back at Dan. "But that scenario fits her as well as anyone. That implicates you, Teri. You were someone in the house. Spur of the moment and all—it fits you perfectly."

It did. The realization was a shock.

"But we know she didn't kill him, Trev. Someone else did," Dan said.

Teri gathered up the dirty plates. Refusing Dan's offer of assistance, she took them back to the camper and began washing. Trevor poured himself another drink.

"So, you've got her story right?" Dan asked. They sat across from each other.

"Yes, I think so." He patted the tape recorder. "She is very lovely."

Dan only nodded.

"But Daniel, is she worth it?"

"Worth what?" His voice fluctuated uncomfortably. "What do you mean?"

"A few days' roll in the hay—"

Dan burst out with, "No! It's not like that," just as Trevor was adding, "—in exchange for many years of incarceration. This is some serious—"

"No. I think you've missed everything here. She's innocent, you have to understand that, and she needs my help. That's all there is to it."

Trevor smirked as he said, "All?" He looked at Dan then twisted around to look at her.

Dan interrupted, "She's very vulnerable, very confused right now. Imagine, the world thinks she killed someone. Put yourself in her position."

Trevor went to top up Dan's glass but Dan pulled it away. Trevor refilled his own.

"Daniel . . ." Trevor started and stopped and started again. "Why are you so certain the lady is innocent? I mean, witness, weapon, prints. Fled the scene. Daniel, how can you be so sure?"

"You don't believe her?"

Trevor grimaced, his head fell a little to one side. "Well, frankly I don't feel certain one way or—"

Dan rose to his feet. "You have to believe her. You have to believe she's innocent or this isn't going to work!"

"Daniel, I think you're the one that is vulnerable, you're the one that is confused. She's taking advantage of you. Daniel, she'll take you down with her."

Dan looked away.

Trevor raised his voice, "All I want to say is, keep some options open. The way these things usually play out . . . well, if you see an opportunity to escape . . ."

Teri hung the towel on the rear view mirror outside the camper. She was close enough to hear.

"Fugitive or criminal, Daniel, it sort of ends the hope of a triumphant return to the mighty Maple Leafs. They were begging—you could name your price."

"You know it never had anything to do with money." Dan stood.

" 'Course not. Though to a mercenary such as myself, money has a certain appeal." Trevor lowered his voice and said with gravity, "It has to do with your father."

Teri glanced from Trevor to Dan.

Trevor stood up. "Front page tomorrow," he spoke with enthusiasm. "Big day for us. Great stuff. I eagerly await riches and fame. And you two, what's next?"

Teri looked away from them and out towards the lake. "I still think I might turn myself in, before anyone gets hurt."

"Not a bad idea." Trevor drained his glass.

She added, "A good lawyer can probably still get Dan out of this mess."

"The underworld's loss could be hockey's gain." Trevor mumbled as he picked up the tape recorder. He rambled on, "Tomorrow's paper will also have a splendid feature on Dan's hockey exploits. I have already put that to bed."

He focused his attention on Teri. "Last year when I was with the *Toronto Sun*, I witnessed every moment Daniel played. The most incredible goaltending ever. Bar none. We ran out of superlatives. I was exhausted just watching him. I lost five pounds every game, better than aerobics. Thrilling."

Dan looked at Teri as if to say, *Don't listen to him, too much to drink.*

By the time Dan had reached the apartment, Trevor had fallen asleep in the back of the van. They had to shake him awake. As he got out of the van both Dan and Teri offered him their thanks. Trevor bowed and said, "I regret, I must bid you adieu. I have a story to write, a deadline to meet, destiny to embrace." He saluted them.

Dan looked into the rear view mirror and pulled away from the curb.

Teri asked, "How well do you know him?"

"Pretty well."

"Where do you know him from?"

"He's a sports reporter." Dan checked the rear view mirror again.

Teri continued to read the notes but said, "You don't know all sports reporters that well, do you?"

"No."

"He's not like you."

Dan checked his rear view again and turned right. "No, he's . . . different. Our paths just seemed to cross several times over the years. He's interesting."

"Interesting, yes."

Then Dan asked, "Are you finding anything?" He turned right again.

"Not much," she said sadly. "Similar to what's in the newspapers. Mr. Hill was a saint. Came out of nowhere and was going to change the world. Everything he did was beyond reproach. Nothing unusual, except . . ." All along this was what she had hoped to be able to do, research. This was what she was good at. But there were no clues here. She had read mystery novels and the clues were supposed to snap together like a jigsaw puzzle. They didn't here. Nothing fit.

"Except what?"

"Well, one thing." Teri hesitated, choosing her words. "Hill had some radical ideas. I think he really was going to shake things up. I think a lot of important and powerful people must have felt threatened by him."

"Enough to kill him?"

"I don't know. People do kill for money and power."

"Yeah, those are popular."

"But I don't know how we could find out."

Dan picked up the cell phone at a stop light and dialed, then flipped on his right turn signal. He jammed the long shift lever into first and released the clutch. The camper lurched forward.

"Where are we going?"

Dan said he didn't know, then spoke into the cell phone, "Tell her I was in to discuss Teri Peterson."

"Peterson?" Excitement bloomed in the secretary's voice. "One moment, please."

Dan fidgeted around and looked into the side mirror. The black Buick was still behind them.

"Mr. Parent?"

"Yes."

"How nice of you to call. Let's—here, I've got your file in front of me. My clerk has been working on it most of the day. Let's see. I was speaking to the district attorney, and he can't offer anything official you understand, but he has suggested that in exchange for an immediate surrender to authorities and a guilty plea, they will not ask for capital punishment and will settle for a life sentence."

Teri had stopped reading through the notes. She moved closer to listen.

Dan nodded. "Hmm, if I see Ms. Peterson, I'll mention it to her. But I don't think she's eager to go to jail at all."

"I can sympathize with that."

"Especially for a murder she didn't commit. Have there been any developments there?"

"Ah, where?"

"Are the police pursuing any other leads, any other suspects?"

"I'm sure they're investigating all possibilities."

"You're sure? But nothing new has turned up?"

"Not that I'm aware of. It's only been a couple of days."

"Ms. Grant, maybe this is just stuff I've seen on television, but you know how they can tell by the angle and direction of the wounds whether the perpetrator was left handed or right, tall or short? Have the police looked into that at all?"

"I really don't know."

"Could you find out?"

"Of course. But Mr. Parent, she should turn herself in, for her own safety. Once she has done that there will be plenty of time for looking into the details. There is a lot of anger out there and—"

"Well, I'll pass that along if I get the chance. Can the police guarantee her safety?"

"Of course. Well, within reason."

After cool pleasantries Dan hung up. He started to dial again. While he listened to the phone ring, he said to her, "I think we've got a problem."

Teri frowned. "Really, just one?"

"Just one new one. There's a black Buick behind us."

"Following us?" She bent to look out her side mirror, but it wasn't angled right.

He nodded.

"Great." Bracing herself, she went to the rear of the van and parted the curtains.

"Hi, Mr. Hedoby?"

"Yes."

"I was in yesterday, asking about Teri Peterson."

"Mr. Parent, I've been hoping you would call. I've found out a few things."

"Like my real name." Dan had never mentioned his name. He had never used it with Ms. Grant either he realized.

"Well, I wouldn't be much of an investigator if I couldn't figure that one out. You do want a good private investigator don't you?"

Dan didn't answer.

"I have some material we should review. Perhaps we could meet."

"Don't think that's possible, at least not right now. Give me the highlights."

"Okay. Nine people are known to have been in the garage-office area that evening. Then in the house were Karen Hill, the children, Ms. Peterson and, during the early part of the evening, one maid." He rattled off the nine names.

Teri wrote the names down.

Teri and Dan made eye contact. Some of the names had the faint ring of familiarity, but one name stood out: Ronald Tasker. She dove into her notes.

Hedoby continued, "It's still early, but none of these people have any motives that we've found. One point of interest is that Mr. Hill arranged a snap press conference for the next day. No one knows what it was for, not even his closest advisors, and that, according to the people I've spoken to, is quite extraordinary."

Dan was impressed. "Okay, that's great. Can you send a copy of your info to Trevor Symes at the *Miami Herald*? He seems to be the only reporter that's questioning Teri's guilt." As he spoke Dan wondered if that was even true. "Hopefully he can do something with it."

"I'll send a copy immediately."

"And can you find out about the knife? Using a common knife seems curious; makes us think that the murder wasn't planned."

"Or perhaps someone wanted it to *look* like it wasn't planned."

"Never thought of that, still—"

"You can't leap to conclusions in this business, and yet, I think it's reasonable to assume this was a spontaneous event. Provocation, anger, reaction."

"Yes. That's what—"

Hedoby interrupted, "I'll focus on what the provocation might have been."

"I don't know if this is possible, but with your connections can you review what Mr. Hill did the last day or two?"

"I've asked to see his appointment book. I should have some news for you in the morning."

They said goodbye. Dan looked at the cell phone to locate the hang up key, then checked the rear view mirror. The sun had slipped beneath the horizon and he could no longer make out the two men inside the car, but the car was still there.

"What are you going to do?"

"Try to lose them, I guess."

"How?"

"I don't know. Won't be easy." Dan was slowly accelerating. "This old crate is a land turtle, just like the sailboat. Beats me. Any ideas?"

Teri looked at the Volkswagen's gas gauge. Trevor had started them with a full tank. "I wonder how much gas they have?"

"Maybe we can find out."

As Dan drove aimlessly, Teri told him about Tasker. "Of all the people in the house that night, he's the most interesting. He was a huge favorite to win the Senate nomination but lost to Hill. How it happened was never clearly explained in the articles I read; there was some kind of scandal at the last minute. But regardless, that's how Hill got started. Prior to that he was an unknown on a small town council and he beat Tasker, who was a congressman and considered an up-and-coming power in the party."

"Was Tasker upset enough at the loss to seek revenge?"

Teri wanted to say yes, but had to say, "No, I don't think so. He's running for Governor now, he's hardly a broken and bitter man out for revenge. You'd think he'd have more important things to do."

"Still, he was there in the house. Why was he there?"

"I've read through all the notes, and there is no indication Hill and Tasker were friends. More like rivals."

"So why was he there?"

Teri shrugged.

"What about the others?"

Teri read out the names, "Mary Kearns, Elliot Farber, Laura Johnston—they were three volunteers helping with the campaign. And Warren Zabbits of course, he practically lived there.'

"Jennie Duffy, a feature writer with the Wall Street Journal. Two people were visiting the office from Greenpeace; Lori Dunston-Withers and John DeLeon, looking for details of Hill's recent environmental announcement, but they left without seeing him. That's interesting but hardly suspicious."

"They all sound like they were there on legitimate business, don't they? But how about Andrew Bash? He's a strategist for Hill's opponent Ron Mercer."

"What was he doing there?" Dan asked. "Would that be normal?"

Teri shrugged. *Would it?* Now, even though they had lots of information to work with, nothing came gift wrapped with a tag that said, *Here's something significant.* Everything seemed perfectly reasonable. She didn't want to give in to frustration—she had to keep focused, keep working. They both did. "I've never heard of Bash, but Mercer, of course," Teri said. "He and Hill held very different views on almost everything. He was running second, well behind in the primaries, but with Hill's death . . ." She shrugged. "Still, I can't believe he'd kill someone to have a shot at the Presidency."

"The Presidency of the United States," Dan uttered the words like they were rolling around in his mind. "Would someone kill to be the President? I think people kill for a lot less."

The Buick hung back, ostensibly minding it's own business. One behind the other they drove into the night, two pair of headlights piercing the dusky twilight, following the empty country road.

Teri asked, "Do you trust Hedoby?"

"Maybe, maybe not."

"Grant?"

"Maybe."

"Trevor?"

"Trevor? Yes."

"There might be a big reward. You don't think that would tempt him?"

"Yeah, it would. But it's not money Trevor wants. He says he does, but not really."

"Oh, what does he want?"

"Fame. Notoriety. Adventure. Bit of excitement. Thrills, that's what gets him cranked up."

They chanced upon an Interstate. Dan took the ramp and headed north. The Buick followed, staying well behind.

Unlike the lonely country road, the Interstate was busy—a multitude of vehicles moving at a frenetic pace.

"He worked for the local paper in Sudbury, where I was playing." It took Teri a moment to realize that Dan was still discussing Trevor. "Then I ran into him again when I played in Las Vegas. In those days things weren't always going well for either of us. Occasionally we'd meet and drown our sorrows. After kicking around in the minors, we both sort of made it to the big time last year. He did a very flattering feature on me. I gave him a few exclusives. When he moved down here to cover the Panthers he told me to look him up. That's it."

"And you trust him?"

"Sure."

"Why?"

"I just do. It's a feeling you get from some people." He looked at her. She understood what he meant, some people you just felt you could trust.

The Volkswagen was careening down the highway as fast as it could go. It shook and vibrated, and yet it was still not going fast enough to collect a ticket from even the most zealous cop; a ticket for going *below* the minimum speed was more likely. The Buick sauntered along in their wake.

"Trevor's a weird guy. He's done a lot of crazy stuff, he's an original, and I just found him interesting. That's all. You don't like him, do you?"

Teri answered, "I shouldn't distract you."

"It's okay. This isn't going to be a high speed chase."

A truck rocketed by and the camper shook in the sudden

draft. Teri cinched up her old style seatbelt. She reached over and tightened up his.

The traffic never let up.

Teri said, "Do you think the police know about the camper? They could be looking for us right now. Maybe we shouldn't just drive all night, hoping they run out of gas."

Dan didn't know what to do. "Let's take a stab at losing them. What do you think?" He glanced into his side view mirror. "If we do, we do. If we don't, we don't."

"That makes sense." Teri nodded. "But how?"

He pressed his foot down to the floor. The camper didn't accelerate.

Teri waited. She watched the speedometer. It didn't budge. "But, how are we—"

A truck passed on the left. Dan swerved out close behind, very close: if they could reach through the windshield they could have grabbed the truck's big steel bumper and held on. Teri caught her breath. She could feel the camper accelerate, sucked forward by the truck. She braced herself and held on to the dash. The van shuddered. She shuddered.

They were almost glued to the back of the eighteen-wheeler. The heavy steel bumper only inches from their eyes.

The Buick pulled out to follow, but one car had slipped in between them. The Buick had to speed up to stay close.

The camper was dragged forward by the truck. The speedometer reached seventy miles an hour, which doesn't seem fast unless you're in an old Volkswagen microbus that can barely reach fifty-five on its own. It felt like they were about to break the sound barrier—the tin walls fluttered, the motor whined, the floor convulsed.

Then they drew alongside a slow moving transport truck. It was just coming onto the interstate, merging with the traffic. The cross winds made matters worse. Dan wrestled with the big steering wheel as the camper lurched from side to side. They were slowly losing their tow. The truck in front was inching away, and the black Buick continued to follow along effortlessly. The other truck, the slow one in the inside lane, was just barely behind them. Dan jerked the steering wheel and changed lanes. He cut in front of the new truck. Teri screamed, the truck horn blared, the driver flashed his high beams again and again.

"Don't kill us," she gasped.

"Try not to."

"Thanks."

Dan muttered, "No problem."

He watched the big grill of the truck up against the rear window of the camper. Teri closed her eyes. The truck's high beams flashed, blazing into the camper, causing Dan to wince and look away from the mirrors.

The car between whizzed by on the left.

The truck driver continued to vent his anger, leaning on the horn over and over. He hugged the camper's back bumper as close as he dared.

Teri yelled, "That guy is really ticked."

Dan's response was to ease slightly off the gas. "I know. I want him to be."

The black Buick appeared.

The camper continued to slow gradually. The truck grill

behind couldn't get any closer, but it did. Teri held her breath, braced for impact.

The driver of the Buick had to decide. He was in the passing lane, driving fast—traffic was heavy and impatient behind him. Suddenly he was alongside the truck's trailer, alongside the cab, alongside the slow moving camper. He could stand on his brakes and hope the car behind him didn't plow into his rear; or he could try to go slow in the fast lane which would infuriate the solid line of speeding cars behind him. He couldn't possibly wedge in between Dan and the truck, there wasn't enough space for an over-weight fly. Before the driver of the Buick could react he was in front of the truck, in front of the Volkswagen, thirty, forty, fifty feet in front.

Dan and Teri watched him pass. "Not many vehicles can go as slow as an old VW microbus," Dan said, relieved. "And you can't follow someone when you're in front of them."

The black car quickly slowed and eased into the right lane directly ahead of Dan and Teri. The gap between the camper and the truck widened and became more comfort-able.

"Well, Trevor doesn't create a good first impression. But he's a good guy, he's harmless. Look at all he's done for us."

Teri didn't argue. She could barely speak. She swallowed and watched the Buick, ahead, and the truck, behind. "He wears a toupee," she muttered.

Dan laughed. "Yeah, he wears a rug. Had a face lift too."

"He's a phony."

Dan shrugged. "I guess. I don't know. He is what he is.

Toupee, face lift: I guess he is a phony, but he doesn't make any bones about it. He'd admit it all with a laugh, so why not? It's his head and his life and his business and he's not hurting anybody doing it. He's a pretty good writer." A moment later Dan added, "Lonely. Drinks like a fish . . . but always a snappy dresser." He looked at Teri, no hint of humor in his face.

Teri hesitated. *Was he serious?* She started to snicker. "He looked downright spiffy, all right."

Dan cracked a smile. "Part of his charm."

He waited until the last second then jerked the camper off the highway onto the ramp of the first exit. Brake lights popped on in the Buick, and it veered over to the shoulder.

"They're going to try backing up to the exit. Take a couple of minutes. With luck they won't guess which way we went."

Dan didn't even slow for the red light, he just shot a gap in the traffic and immediately got back on the highway again heading in the opposite direction.

"Strange guy, but I do trust him." He was heading south. They both watched the car lights behind them. "Remember, you didn't like me at first either."

" 'Course not." Teri glanced over and snapped, "So what's your point?" She let him twist in the wind a little. Then she said with a snicker and a smile, "Just kidding."

Again the Volkswagen was rocked and buffeted as a truck roared past. The harsh glare of headlights invaded the little camper from every direction. Brightly lit billboards made their silent announcements.

"Where to?"

Dan shrugged. "Bahamas?"

Teri groaned.

Dan added, "These old Volkswagens float. Didn't you know? They're air-tight. Just rig a sail out of sheets and we're on our way."

Teri scowled.

After a chuckle, he said, "Unfortunately, I think we have to ditch her."

"I know, but I've made the bed." It was such a cozy looking bed, with fresh sheets and soft pillows, and even a down, filled duvet.

A *Days Inn* billboard flashed by. What were the chances they could just check into a motel? Could they risk it?

"Maybe we could find an out-of-the-way place to park for the night and ditch her in the morning? Somewhere where we can just park and sleep. I'm tired. I'm to tired to think."

A *Country Kitchen* billboard. *Texaco. Sunken Gardens. Cracker Barrel.*

"Someplace where there is nobody around." Teri leaned back. The seat was more like a perch. She put her feet up on the dash. There was just darkness, bright lights and billboards to look at. Dan kept driving.

"Trevor said they're begging for you back? I thought you were injured."

"I was injured," he said, "now I'm retired."

"I thought you were trying to impress me. How come you never bragged about being this super hockey hero?"

"Trevor is given to exaggeration—it's part of his job description. In the media you're always either a hero or a bum, there's nothing in between. There isn't much of a story in being an average Joe, and yet most players *are* average Joes."

"Are you an average Joe?"

"It's what I've always aspired to be."

Dan took an exit ramp.

"Still, you could have mentioned it."

"Are you a hockey fan?"

"No, but—"

"Ever seen a game?"

"No, but . . ."

He shrugged.

Undaunted Teri added, "I still would have been impressed."

Dan stopped at the top of the ramp. "I was saving it. Going to tell you at just the right moment."

Teri snickered.

"Are we safe here, do you think?" Teri sat on the foot of the bed facing the windshield. She looked over her shoulder to Dan.

He was lying flat on his back already on the short bed, under the duvet. "Guess we'll find out." His feet hung over the end and dangled free.

She mused, "Are we safe anywhere?"

Tonight they were anything but alone. Parked close to a chain link fence, they were in the furthest corner of a crowded truck stop. Outside dozens of big rigs were parked. Some sat empty while the drivers went inside to eat, others had sleepers in the back of the cabs. Most of the trucks left their diesel engines idling. The motors throbbed and shook the air.

"Who do you think they were?" Teri asked. She washed her face in the little sink.

Dan shook his head. "I don't know."

"Same guys that visited us on the boat?"

"Maybe. Probably."

Teri put down the towel. She looked at him. Her eyes slipped down his long lean form. She spied his bare feet protruding and chuckled nervously, "You have nice feet."

"Thank you. Probably my best feature."

She giggled and put her hand on his feet. "You don't fit." Embarrassed, she wrapped the sheet around his feet.

"Thanks."

"Well," Teri said standing up. "I know you like to sleep with your feet covered." She reached out and turned off the last light. The parking lot was lit with tall towers of florescent lights that bore through the thin curtains, illuminating the cabin in a ghostly hue.

A hundred yards away two men sat in a black Buick and watched the light go out.

Teri was exhausted. The small bed promised a level of comfort that she'd craved all day. She crawled in beside him.

"Down to nine suspects," he said.

Teri nodded, before adding, "Unless someone snuck in off the street.

The diesel fumes were oppressive. Dan reached up and slid the side window closed. "I keep thinking it has something to do with Tasker."

"Or Bash."

The bed felt scrumptious.

"Or maybe one of the others, who knows? Maybe they were hired by some big business or special interest group."

Nine was still eight too many.

Chapter Eight

Even in an empty sea of asphalt, Harvey Stoad always made a point of parking his big rig in the farthest corner of the lot. Most workdays the only exercise he got were these long walks to the truck stop for breakfast. He left his motor running and climbed down beside the little camper. Harvey appreciated the quirky old Volkswagen microbus— it was in mint condition. He strolled once around then started to leave, but something compelled him to glance back—there was a green garden hose on the exhaust. It curved up from the tailpipe and fed into the trunk. *The exhaust was being directed back into the van?* That stopped him.

After a long thoughtful pause, he tapped lightly on the window. "Hey." He whispered, "Anybody in there?"

Dan and Teri shot up at once, then held still to listen. They could see the shadow of a man move on the curtain.

"You okay in there?"

Holding their breath, they looked at each other. Dan responded, "Good morning," not knowing what else to say.

"I just, ah, wanted to make sure you were all right, because . . ."

Dan reached out and opened the door a crack. He slipped out and shut the door quickly behind him.

There was only one man, a portly man in loose green work pants and a T-shirt, non-threatening. "I, ah, saw that hose. Thought you'd . . . well, you know."

Dan stared dumbly at the man.

Harvey Stoad asked, as he backed up to the rear of the van, "That hose, what you got that there for?"

Dan looked. He saw the garden hose looped from the tail pipe into the engine compartment. It was sealed up with duct tape. "I don't . . ." He shrugged.

Harvey Stoad squinted at him as if he was dangerous, maybe a death cult kind of guy. He didn't get too close. "Trying to kill yourself? It ain't going to work. Old Volkswagens—they got a rear engine compartment, all sealed up from the rest of the vehicle. This sort of suicide plan would work just fine on one of those new minivans—not that I'm suggesting anything."

"I didn't . . . I . . . I don't know how that hose got there." Dan struggled to rip off a piece of tape, and wispy gray soot wafted out. He pulled out the hose and looked at it. Then he opened the engine compartment, and a thin gray film covered the motor. He fingered the dust.

The two men stared at each other at a loss for words. Harvey Stoad said, stumbling over his words, "Life is . . .

you know, tough sometimes but this, this is not . . ." The trucker glanced down at his brown work boots.

Dan looked at the engine compartment. He couldn't figure it out. The truck driver was right, it looked like an attempted suicide. The hose had been hooked up to pump carbon monoxide into the van.

Then Harvey said, "You know guy, you should get some help. Professional help. You should."

Dan still couldn't think of anything to say. He was baffled. The hose and engine compartment were covered in very fine exhaust dust.

"Well . . ." Harvey added. He was hungry, and if somebody wanted to kill himself, well, that had nothing to do with him. He felt bad, but he'd done his bit. Wagging his head, Harvey started to walk away.

"Excuse me," Dan called after him. "Do you know— would the van run like this?" The question in his mind was, *when was this done? Where did the exhaust dust come from?*

Harvey took one step back. "Screw up the compression something awful. You could idle maybe, that's it. Pump the gas and you'd sure as heck stall."

"So I couldn't drive down the highway?"

"Heck no. No way." Harvey looked at the dust. "But that, that looks like a lot of idling. You leave the engine running all night?"

"No," Dan answered. "Not at all." It couldn't be from *his* engine. He called out his thanks as Harvey slipped away.

This must have been done last night, Dan concluded, *but not by the VW's engine.* Someone attached the exhaust from another car and pumped the van full of carbon monoxide, or at least they thought they did. They didn't know that the old Volkswagen had a rear engine compartment. Then they cut off the hose and looped it back to the camper's exhaust, to make it look like suicide.

Teri leaned cautiously out the door. Dan explained,

"Someone tried to kill us last night, tried to make it look like attempted suicide."

Teri didn't try to understand. She just said, "Let's get out of here."

The Volkswagen trundled onto the Interstate. Teri handed Dan a bagel with cream cheese and a mug of orange juice, then plopped down beside him and, resting her feet on the dash, she delved back into Trevor's stack of notes.

Dan was talking to Anne Grant on the cell phone. "But it's got to be the real murderer who is trying to kill us. It's not the police, and it's not someone looking for a reward. They tried to make it look like suicide."

Anne asked, "Give me a description."

"Well, I didn't see them. But two guys followed us yesterday in a black Buick."

"Are those the guys?"

"I think so. But I'm not positive."

"Did you get their plates?"

Dan snapped, "No."

Ms. Grant said softly, "That's not a lot for the police to work with."

She was right. "But they tried to make it look like suicide. It's not some angry citizen, it's not some vigilante. It's someone who's trying to shut us up. They could have called the police. They could have murdered us while we slept, but they went to elaborate lengths to fabricate something that would look like a suicide. Why?"

He waited a moment, and when Ms. Grant did not respond he added, "I'll tell you why. They don't want any loose ends. They don't want anyone running around wondering who would've killed us and why. They don't want anyone talking conspiracy, or accomplices. They want the world to think that Teri is just some lone nut case who killed Hill, and then herself, for reasons she took to the grave with her. That would be the end of it. All over. Closed up neat. I think this *is* a conspiracy. Probably some big and powerful, business group terrified of Hill becoming President killed him."

Anne waited until she was certain he was finished. "You may be right, but really, you have to turn yourselves in. Next time you might not be so lucky."

Dan added, "Okay, thanks. Bye." He hung up.

"She's just doing her job." Teri had never seen Dan so tense. "And I think she's right."

Dan's eyes stared ahead at the traffic. He began to nod. "I know," he replied thoughtfully, "and that really bugs me too."

A black sedan pulled up behind them. The driver examined the red and white microbus. Teri tried to watch without looking. Every person in every car seemed to stare. Teri hoped it was because the Volkswagen was so distinctive. Other than having a fridge and a bed in the back it wasn't the best choice for fugitives; unlike many cars, it didn't fade into the background.

"Dan?"

"Hmm?"

"You okay?"

"Just great," he said angrily.

Teri shook her head. Reaching over, she put her hand on his knee and murmured, "It seems like something has happened to you. Some sort of fundamental change—you're different today."

"Me?" He frowned.

Her eyes reached out to caress his face. "Tense. Worried. Starting to come apart at the seams."

Dan was taken aback. For a moment he was speechless. But he had felt a little odd; things had changed. "People are trying to *kill* you."

"I know. I'm getting used to it."

Dan snorted despite himself.

Teri added, "They're trying to kill you too, and will, unless we keep thinking calmly."

There was so much at stake—it was becoming hard to breathe.

"You can't change. You're my rock, you're unflappable Dan. If we're going to get out of this, I need you to stay the way you were. You know, 'I don't think I think like most people.' "

Her comment provoked a reluctant smile. Shaking his head in amazement, he said, "This is going to take some getting used to."

"Regrets?"

"No. None."

She leaned over and kissed him quickly on the cheek. "You didn't shave this morning."

"I was kind of preoccupied."

Another black car went by. This one slowed beside them, and without looking Teri could feel the driver staring. "If we see those guys again we've got to figure out a way to grab them. That's the only way. Find who they're working for."

"Then what? Even if we know who killed Hill, we still have to prove it."

"I know." It'd be a huge step, but it only illustrated what a long way they had to go.

Dan thought about that. "I'd just as soon not see them again."

Teri could appreciate that idea. Another black car approached. Out of the corner of her eye she watched it pass. It was driving her crazy—there were too many black cars. She gave up watching for them. Leaning back again, she closed her eyes. "I never thought I'd say it, but I'm thinking maybe Bahamas."

Dan laughed as he dialed the cell phone. He'd just said hello, when Clay Hedoby launched into: "Look, you've got to ditch that Volkswagen."

"What?"

"The Volkswagen van you're driving. I can hear that little air-cooled engine over the phone. The police have a tip: an old red and white VW camper. An anonymous tip: you're in a camper at a truck stop on I-95. It's going out to all officers and the media, right now."

Teri jammed the bulk of her bagel into her mouth and stuffed the notes back into her satchel, then wriggled into the belly of the van and hauled out two knapsacks.

Hedoby ordered, "Ditch it, quick. Then call me. I've got stuff for you."

Across the median there was a highway patrol car. It was going fast the other way.

Next exit, Dan pulled off the Interstate.

This time it was Teri's idea. When they stopped for a traffic light there was a sign in a window, *Last minute cruise deals*. They had made it through a downtown section of Fort Lauderdale and were driving by a strip of small night spots and restaurants. It looked sleepy and subdued in the early morning light.

Turning onto a side street, Dan entered a small municipal lot. Pulling up the parking brake, he turned off the engine, jumped out, grabbed a knapsack, slammed the door and locked it. Together they started to jog away from the camper.

They approached the travel agency, walked by the store front, surreptitiously peeked in as they strolled past, then stopped and looked back.

"Well, what do you think?"

"I only saw one person in there."

Teri answered, "Yes, me too," then added, "Look." She pointed at the rolled up newspaper by the door. "She hasn't checked her paper yet. She might not know, at least not about you."

A moment later they entered the store. Dan approached the woman and she held up her left hand like a stop sign, meanwhile the fingers of her right hand kept furiously tapping the corner of the keyboard. "Oh," she exclaimed. She never looked up from her computer screen. "No, no."

Dan waited.

"No!"

On the radio in the background, Jimmy Buffet lamented about, *Wasting away again in Margaritaville*, and Teri stood by the door, back to the agent, perusing a rack of brochures.

Sondra—Dan read the name tag on her blue blazer—was young, an attractive woman who paid attention to her appearance. Her blond hair was pulled back in a loose chignon. She wore a simple business-like cream colored skirt and a navy blue blazer.

Dan leaned forward and checked out the screen.

She kept tapping the keys faster and faster until suddenly she stopped. With a scrunched up fist she pounded the top of the computer screen. "I almost had it. I am never going to get to the next level." Looking up, she finally made eye contact with Dan.

He said he was sorry.

"Oh, it's not your fault." Her pout vanished, and her long eye lashes flickered. "Now then, what can I do for you all?"

"Are there any cruises leaving today?"

"Why of course. Most days there's at least one."

"Your sign in the window says you have last minute cruise deals?"

Nodding, Sondra punched one key, paused, then launched a flurry of keystrokes.

"Spur of the moment thing. Won a little money at the dog track, thought we'd celebrate." He looked over to Teri and Sondra followed his eyes, but just for an instant.

"Let me see here. The *Sun Goddess* leaves this evening for a fourteen-day cruise through the Panama Canal to Los Angeles, stopping in—"

"I don't think we won that much, any others?"

Sondra checked her screen. *"Sea Fantasy*, leaves for a three-day trip to Nassau and Horizon Key, at six thirty."

Dan turned to Teri. "Oh, that sounds nice, what do you think?"

"How much is it?"

Sondra produced the appropriate brochure from a rack behind her desk and passed it over to Dan, while she described the cabin choices and prices. Teri handed her the money just as Jimmy finished singing.

Dan began to count out the money. Sondra began to fill out the ticket.

The radio carried on: *"Unconfirmed reports say two people fitting the description of fugitives Teri Peterson and Dan Parent—"*

Sondra hadn't been actively listening, but Dan could see a spark of curiosity kindle in her eyes. She hesitated. He looked over at Teri. Teri was listening as well. Panic was in the air.

"—are still in the south Florida area—"

Sondra glanced over at the radio.

It would be too obvious to turn off the radio, too obvious just to make noise . . . Dan said, "On level seven, have you tried looking in the closet first?"

"The closet?"

"As soon as you come in the room, there's a closet on the right." He had her attention. "And if you push on the wall there's a secret passageway, so you don't have to deal with the grubbies until after you find the cloak of invisibility in the dungeon."

"Really? I've tried so many times to get past them."

"Nobody has told you about the closet and the secret passage?"

"No."

"It's easier if you have the cloak."

"Well, I guess so, if you're invisible."

"Stay tuned to Sun ninety-nine-point-nine for up-to-the-moment coverage of this and other—"

"Thanks. I can't wait to try it again. Now, all I need is your names."

"Anderson," Dan said. "Mr. And Mrs. Derek Anderson."

Sondra took the money and handed over the tickets. By then the radio station had moved onto college basketball scores.

Dan plucked up the tickets and they quickly left. Once out into the bright sun and muggy heat, Teri muttered under her breath, "Pretty smooth, but they'll broadcast the report again."

"I know."

"What then?"

"Hopefully she'll be engaged in mortal combat with the grubbies."

As they walked on, they wandered into a residential area with more black asphalt than vegetation, and more water than either. Every home was on a canal and large boats competed with the houses for vertical dominance.

Teri asked, "You figure we'll just stroll on board and no one will notice?"

"That's hard to believe, isn't it?"

"Yes."

"Got a better idea?"

"No."

"Me neither."

"We should try to think of one."

Dan nodded.

Chapter Nine

"**S**till at large?" Teri pointed at the newspaper headlines. "What does that mean, 'at large'?"

"Look at this," Dan showed her a colored pie chart on
the second page of the paper. "They did a poll. Thirty-eight
percent of Americans think you're a psychopath, forty-two
percent think you're part of a special interest group, eleven
percent think it was a crime of passion, and nine percent
say they don't know. No one says you're innocent or might
be innocent—it wasn't even offered as an option."

There was another pie chart below the first. "Here
they've broken down who you might be working for! Eight
percent say for the tobacco industry. Five percent say the
National Rifle Association, a government agency! Organized crime! The oil industry. Communists. Pro-Arab in-
terests . . . They've got everybody here."

Teri took one of the other papers from under his arm. "Is that Trevor's paper you've got? What does he say?"

"This article shows there are lots of other people who may have had a motive."

"That's good," she said as she looked for Trevor's article. "But which group? Which individual? How do we prove it?"

The road rose for the Los Olas bridge over the Intra-Coastal waterway. As Dan and Teri walked up the rise the lights began to flash, and a horn blared. There was a pause at this point to make sure that all traffic was clear of the center of the bridge. Then the two spans began to tilt up.

Dan and Teri reached the barrier, a long metal pole. Dan lowered his paper and glanced at the sailboat waiting to pass through—nobody he knew. He turned his back and sat on the rim of the guardrail. Teri moved in beside him, and they began to read Trevor's article.

"You were supposed to phone Hedoby back," Teri reminded him.

Dan nodded and took out the phone.

"Okay," Hedoby immediately began to run through his notes. "I've interviewed almost everyone in the house at the time of the murder. They all say they were there in the pit, they can vouch for each other. But they each have a little cubicle and they can come and go and nobody notices. I mean, just to go to the washroom they have to leave the pit and go halfway into the house. Anyone could slip out for a couple of minutes and no one would know.

"By the way, I still haven't talked to Mrs. Hill. She's under doctors care."

Hedoby continued, "Another thing, I called CNN. I

spoke to the person who actually took the call from Hill, and she was certain it was Hill himself who called to arrange the press conference. He called just after eight o'clock. That's about an hour or so before the murder. No one at the station knows exactly what the announcement was going to be, but Hill said it would be newsworthy. He didn't say anything else.

"As you instructed, I passed everything over to your friend Trevor Symes. He's covered it all quite well in today's paper."

Dan interrupted, "We're reading it now."

"Good."

"That's great, thanks Clay." Dan told him about the incident the previous night, then added, "I know you can't—I mean I know a black Buick isn't a lot to go on. I just thought I'd let you know."

Hedoby agreed that the more he knew, the better. "One of the local detectives assigned to this case is my old partner. She's going to let me see Hill's appointment book this afternoon. I believe, like you do, that it was a spur of the moment decision to murder Hill, so something recent had to have happened. I'm going to go back over what Hill had been doing, who he'd been seeing the last day or two."

"That's great."

"And we have to find out what his announcement was going to be, and why his troops didn't know anything about it. Surely his wife must have known. I'm going to try to talk to her." Hedoby sounded in a hurry, so Dan didn't interrupt. "So, read the article, then give me a call in a couple of hours. We can discuss it then if you'd like."

"Clay," Dan started. "You've been talking to the police. Where do they think we are?"

"I'm sorry, man, I can't help you with that."

"What do you mean?"

"That's aiding a fugitive. It's breaking the law. I'd lose my license. Besides, I have great respect for the law."

"But you told us they knew about the van."

"That was common knowledge when I told you. CNN was about to run the story."

"You've been helping us all along."

"Sure, as much as I can, but not to escape. I've been helping you with your investigation into the actual murder. That's perfectly legit. It's all you hired me to do. That's all I *can* do." Hedoby paused. "You're fugitives. I told you, I've still got a lot of friends on the force. From time to time they're a great help to me. I can't stab them in the back."

"Do you tell them where we are?"

"I don't *know* where you are. But anything I do figure out . . . yeah, I tell them. I have to. Man, I can't help fugitives evade the police."

The bridge tender started to blow his horn as Dan clicked off. They began to walk again.

"That guy has got interesting scruples."

Dan nodded. "He works for us, but only on the investigation into the murder. He's perfectly willing to tell the police anything he finds out about us. Makes you stop and think, doesn't it?"

From the top of the bridge they could see the sea and the wide golden sweep of Fort Lauderdale beach and the hordes of people.

"Makes you wonder who else he might sell information to."

"Resourceful guy."

"Our leak?"

Teri never paid much attention to the sports section, but this time it caught her eye.

"Most valuable player in the Stanley Cup playoffs?" She read on, Trevor didn't make this up—a trophy for the most valuable player in the playoffs. You either got that or you didn't. Eyes still on the page, she burst out with, "Considered one of the greatest goaltenders of all time!"

"Now, *that's* Trevor embellishing." He didn't look up, he just kept skimming through Trevor's notes as they walked along the beachfront highway.

"You didn't cheat or anything, did you?"

"Cheat?"

"I don't know. I don't know anything about hockey. Is it rigged? Like wrestling?"

He scoffed.

She read some more and muttered, "I just think it's weird that you have an accomplished something like this and you didn't even mention it. It's a shame that you can't play anymore."

He nodded. "Yeah, right. It's also a shame that you can't finish your Ph.D. But what's *really* a shame is this murder thing—solve that and you can get your life back."

"And you, you can return to the Toronto Maple Leafs?"

Dan shrugged.

"I'd like to see you play hockey," she said simply. She

found the water bottle on his pack, opened it and took a swig.

"Maybe there's something in here," Dan said pointing to the notes.

"Nothing much. I've read every word. At least there's nothing that stands out, nothing that I can find." Then she mumbled and tapped the sports section. "But there's a lot more in here. You're still hiding something from me, Mr. Hockey Star. Why are you doing that? What was it Trevor said about your father?"

He winced. It was almost imperceptible, but she noticed. Her constant talk of his hockey past rankled, so she decided to let it drop for now.

Dan kept skimming the pages. "There has got to be something in here. This, essentially, is the guy's life. If someone had a logical reason to murder him, there should be a hint somewhere in all this."

Two girls in bikinis buzzed by on roller blades. The beach was packed. The road was bumper-to-bumper.

Dan announced, "Hill jumped from city councilor in Wilkes-Barre, Pennsylvania to run for the senate."

"Yes," Teri concurred. "I'm from Scranton, almost neighbors. I think that helped me get the job."

Dan kept reading. "Originally a high school teacher."

Teri nodded. She knew this. She'd been over it all in her mind so many times it had become meaningless. "So was his wife, Karen. She wasn't at all keen on his political quest."

"Do you think—"

"No. She didn't. She really loved him, I'm sure of that. That's one name we can cross off the list. She was proud of him, just worried about all the sacrifices the family would have to make. And she was terrified something like this might happen. She told me once about how he was stepping on so many powerful toes, and it worried her."

"Whose toes?" He thought about it as he flipped through the pages.

"But if it was a special interest group, if it was an assassination, then it was premeditated, not spontaneous. Hill's murder wasn't planned."

"I forgot that."

A policeman on a bicycle rode by. He was wearing shorts and high socks. Everywhere you looked there was throngs of people and police.

"He came out of nowhere," Dan mumbled. "Won the senate nomination in a huge upset. Then won the senate seat, helped by a general increase in party support. Then his innovative policies started to make him sort of a folk hero."

"That and the fact that he was scrupulously honest."

"A saint. Out to change the world, look at all these policy statements. He made lots of powerful enemies. But it wasn't a planned murder."

She said simply, "I don't know."

They reached the end of the beach. The road swung up onto the causeway.

"Do you think we'll be able to get onto the cruise ship?"

He shrugged. "Might be another lucky streak, might as well ride it out as far as we can."

"Lucky streak? You believe that stuff, don't you?"

"What can I say? I'm a goalie . . . used to be a goalie. I wore the same underwear for three months."

"Charming. The playoffs last year, was that just a lucky streak?"

Dan didn't answer.

"Is that why you quit hockey, you think you've had your lucky streak? You figure you can't ever play like that again?"

"Can't. Absolutely impossible. I don't know how it happened the first time." He shook his head. "Every guess I made was right. Pucks just kept hitting me. On every shot it was like I gambled and won the lottery, shot after shot, game after game."

"Well then what happened? Did you lose your lucky underwear? Did another goalie steal it?" Teri added the question, "How many games?"

"Twelve to end the season, nineteen in the playoffs."

"Thirty-one games of luck?"

"It was unbelievable. I can't play like that again."

"And you don't want to tamper with the 'Dan the magic man,' mystique."

"Should I? I can be a bum again in a hurry, it's the nature of sports. Then it all becomes a fluke."

"You want to go down in the books as the mystery man, appeared out of nowhere, performed the impossible, vanished into the night." Chuckling mournfully, she said, "Right now, I'm going down in the history books as a heinous villain. Murdered the saint, then vanished. We'll be quite a pair."

The road began to rise. There was another bascule bridge ahead. There was no longer a crowd to disappear into.

"I don't believe it. You, my fearless knight in shining armor, are scared."

He shrugged.

"You're scared to play hockey and you're scared to crack those books. Scared that with all the schooling you missed, you won't be able to hack it. You're a coward."

"You seem surprised. I've always known I was a coward."

Waving her arms wide, she said, "But all this?"

Dan said, "I didn't do any of this because I get a rush out of danger. I'd much rather get to know you over dinner and a movie. Right now, I'm terrified. Terrified I might lose you. It was a lot easier when I was convinced there was no future for us."

She smiled. "Now you think there might be?"

"Maybe." He closed his eyes. "I don't know."

"You don't know?"

"Sometimes I think, you're feeling alone and frightened. You need somebody and I'm here and handy, and that's all there is to it. I have become your, 'any port in a storm.' "

"That's not true."

"Let's face the facts here. It wasn't exactly love at first sight for you, was it? If you had an opportunity to get away from me you would have taken it. How many times did you want to just jump overboard and swim away?"

She had. She couldn't deny it. Fool that she was, she'd been scared of him. Terrified of him! Nothing could seem more ridiculous now.

Dan carried on, "Picture this: we're in a bar, and I sidle up alongside you and ask if I can buy you a drink . . . you, what? Scream?"

"I don't go into bars."

"There we go. Enough said. Do you go to hockey games?"

She shook her head.

"Then we never meet. We live separate lives."

Teri thought seriously not only about what he said, but about the underlying truth he was driving at. "Maybe you're right, under normal circumstances we would never have met. But we did. We did meet. So?"

First thin white smoke, then the top deck of the cruise ship came into view. Three enormous cruise ships were docked at the port.

Teri continued to think about what he'd said. She looked at him. He was not at all what she had spent twenty four years of her life dreaming of. It was still a shock to see him. He did scare her in a peculiar way that made her tremble, but it was a happy tremble. And she didn't truly understand her feelings, she could admit that.

Dan said, "Tell you what, we get through this, we'll try a regular date, okay? See how that goes."

"You're on."

"Great, I'm looking forward to it. Now all we have to do is figure out who killed Hill, and how to prove it."

"Piece of cake."

Chapter Ten

Dan and Teri continued to march up the back of the causeway. Thick heat radiated up from the asphalt and the hoods of slow moving cars. Ahead the ships shimmered in the sun, like a mirage.

"So? What do you think?" Teri asked. It was hard to believe they could just stroll onto a cruise ship and sail out of the country when the town they were in was like an armed camp.

A few more steps and they could see the palm trees and the convention center, and the white concrete of the parking garages. Finally they could make out two police cars blocking the entrance to the port authority. The police were stopping to check every vehicle that came to enter.

"Got any other ideas?" she asked as their pace slowed. "What do you think?"

He shook his head. "I don't know."

147

Dan stepped over the guardrail. They walked halfway down the hill and sat in the high, dry grass. The cars and taxis were thoroughly searched, even the trunks were popped open. Express buses from the airport and delivery vans received only the most perfunctory inspection, but how would they get on one of those? Two men sat in a boat fishing, tied to the fenders under the bridge. One sailboat circled impatiently, waiting for an opening.

Teri laid back in the parched grass. She closed her eyes and rested. They waited.

It amazed her that in the midst of this hectic, desperate flight to freedom there continued to be occasions of strange calmness. They were just lazing in the sun swishing away bugs, craving decisive action but wondering what to do. If they could just get to their cabin on the ship without drawing any attention, that would buy them a couple of days at least. A couple more days and they might actually figure out who really killed Mr. Hill. It was the first time she thought they might actually be able to do it. Perhaps some part of her brain was trying to tell her something; maybe the clues were all there, they just had to assemble them. She tried again, but her mind continued to travel down the same well-worn path that ended with the same conclusion: she didn't know.

The horn blew. The traffic stopped. The bridge began to open and the sailboat crept into the maw and out of sight. From the other direction two boats emerged: *Carpe Diem* with Neville at the helm, then the bright red hull of *Cherry Pie*. Turning for the ocean, they were almost instantly assailed by two police boats. Dan watched as the three boats were searched then allowed to proceed on their way. He watched the mast tips pass beyond the palm trees and slowly recede out into the ocean.

"You know," Teri said, "I don't want to just run away and become a fugitive." She stopped to sort things through in her mind. "I want to learn who killed Mr. Hill. I mean, it's not right that the murderer can just get away. I don't want to go jail. I don't want to get killed, but I really want to catch the murderer for Mr. Hill's sake, and for Karen's and the kid's. That's one of the reasons I don't want to go to jail."

"And me?"

"What?"

"You don't want to go to jail because that would mean we'd be parted, right? You forgot that bit."

She didn't have to look at him to know he was teasing. "Yeah. Sure. That too," she said offhandedly.

A breeze was yanking the thin white smoke from the stacks and out to sea.

Dan had been running through various avenues of escape and considered the catamarans for rent on the beach. It was a perfect southwest wind, a beautiful reach all the way to Bimini. But a southwest wind is usually very temporary in this latitude. He knew it would quickly clock to the west and build. There was a front coming, a norther. You could feel heaviness building in the air. And he didn't want to be out there in a catamaran in a storm—probably not a good time to cross in a modest sailboat, either. Neville must be trying to make a quick zip to Bimini and beat the front, or more likely just nipping down to Miami and the anchorage at the harbor.

He looked at the *Sea Fantasy*. A big cruise ship wouldn't

have any trouble in a storm. He felt the tickets in his pocket. *How to get aboard?*

Teri felt her stomach rumble. "Maybe they'll take a supper break."

"That'd be nice. It'd be nice if they left even for a few minutes." There were restaurants in the plaza across the highway in front of a marina. That caused him to think of boats again . . . maybe they could steal a boat, a speed boat. He remembered the police patrol boats. That wouldn't work.

"You know," Dan rolled to his haunches and stood up. He was looking for something. There was a sign for Pier 66 marina. "Maybe we should encourage them to leave." He pulled out the cell phone.

Hedoby told Dan about the meeting between Tasker and Hill. "I spoke to Tasker. He accused Hill of planting a malicious rumor to gain the senate nomination back in Pennsylvania."

Dan asked, "Could *he* have killed him?"

"I doubt it. He said himself Hill's murder just makes it more difficult for him to uncover the truth. He went to see Hill to give him a chance to come clean—next thing he knows, the guy's murdered. I think Tasker is shocked and genuinely upset."

"Well, thanks. I wanted to let you know, we're going to be out of touch for a while. We've got a boat, a speed boat. We're at Pier 66 marina gassing up, and as soon as it gets darker, we're out of here." Dan carried on, "Probably run down the coast and try to get lost in the Keys . . . then I don't know."

Hedoby interrupted, "Dan, you know, you shouldn't tell me this."

Dan quipped back, "Hey, Clay, I'm not worried. I've got faith in you, man. I'll be in touch." He hung up.

They continued to sit in the dry grass. Their cruise ship waited. But nothing happened until two police boats silently raced in from the cut. They roared under the bridge kicking up a heavy wake, then two police cars that formed the roadblock drove away, quickly, lights flashing, but again no sirens. Behind them, they heard the police cars rattle over the bridge. Two more police cars swept by at high speed.

Dan and Teri stood up and swiftly walked over the bridge. The roadblock suddenly gone, traffic flooded into Port Everglades. Once again the fugitives were swallowed up by the crowd.

Up and down the gangplank, all around Dan and Teri flowed cresting waves of excited chatter. Dan and Teri were silent so they could hear when the conversations switched away from the imminent splendors of shipboard life.

"They're here, cornered at a marina."

"Here?"

"Who?"

"Just on the other side of the bridge."

"That girl who murdered Hill."

"What bridge?"

"So that's why the police took away that roadblock."

People stood on toes. People pointed. People nudged forward impatiently, eager to get board the ship.

Dan and Teri exchanged glances.

"Well, you can't see the bridge from down here."

"How far? Why don't we hear sirens?"

"Police don't want to spook them. But there's a chopper."

"There's another one."

"I wonder if we'll hear gunshots."

"From the upper deck we might be able to see something."

The throng shuffled forward. Dan and Teri had no interest in witnessing the arrest of any fugitives—they were more concerned with the stewards. Once they got beyond the check-in, they felt they'd be safe. The roadblock had put the crew of the cruise ship behind schedule and had resulted in a crush of passengers eager to board. They were pestering the harried staff with questions about the rumors; where exactly was the marina? Could they see the marina from the bow? Was it true, had they heard anything new? There was an excited crowd building along the railing at the bow on the upper promenade and noisy helicopters thundering overhead.

Dan and Teri reached the top of the ramp and entered into a tiny portal. It was cool and dark. The line of passengers curved around a long wooden reception desk. A steward waved them forward.

This is it, Teri thought. *If we can pull this off we'll be safe.*

The steward took the ticket from Dan's hand. As he briskly and mechanically examined the ticket, he asked, "And may I take an imprint of a credit card, sir?" Meanwhile another steward standing beside him punched the name into a computer and flipped through a rack of manila envelopes and extracted one that said, *Mr. and Mrs. Anderson, Sapphire deck, cabin S310.*

"Um," Dan began. "I don't have a credit card."

The first steward had ripped out one page from the ticket, and hesitated as he began to hand back the remaining pages.

Teri grimaced and snickered with gusto, making certain to catch the eye of both stewards as she made a snip-snip motion with her fingers. The two men looked slightly embarrassed.

"Is that a problem?" Dan asked.

"Not really sir. We prefer a credit card imprint but your ticket is already paid for. It just means you won't be able to charge anything to your cabin." He punched in a series of commands to the computer. "There we go."

"You will need identification to disembark in Nassau and to return to the United States." Dan flourished the passport.

The other steward handed the envelope to Dan. "You are up one deck, sir, elevators behind you, staircase ahead on the left." The other steward nodded, smiled and said, "Thank you for choosing Fantasy Cruise lines, and I hope you enjoy your voyage," then turned to the next passenger.

It was that easy. They walked away from the reception counter and entered a lobby area. Teri barely suppressed an urge to leap into the air and shout with joy. The dining room spread out beside them, there was a small pizzeria ahead, a patisserie across from that and the entrance to the nightclub beyond. They quickly set out to find their cabin. Up one flight of wide stairs and they were on the Sapphire deck, half-way down the next corridor they found cabin S310.

"This is incredible, I can't believe we made it." She danced around, peeking into the tiny washroom and closet. Twin beds extended from one wall, and at the end of the small cabin there was a desk, a chair, a television and a small window.

His gaze followed her around the room and when it settled upon her face she felt a shiver of pure joy.

"The lucky streak continues."

She laughed and leapt up into his arms, giddy with relief and delight. She kissed him and said again, "I can't believe we made it."

They'd discovered a new sanctuary. No longer were there only scant stolen moments available to them—they had days.

She closed her eyes and sighed. "I'm staying right here until we reach Nassau." A vast mansion could not have felt more sumptuous than their little cabin.

Dan asked, "And do what?"

"Work," she answered

"Sounds great."

"Mostly work. We've got a lot of work ahead of us—this isn't a vacation."

"No, it's not a vacation," he agreed, then murmured, "But it sure feels like one."

"This just buys us some time. We still have to . . ." She was unable to say, *determine who killed Hill.* She'd said it so often it was becoming meaningless.

But Dan said it for her. "Figure out who killed Hill."

"Yes, if we want this to be more than a little interlude.

We aren't in the clear yet. Do you have a trick ready to clear customs in Nassau?"

Teri began a list of people in the house at the time of the murder. She stared at the list she had written: Tasker, Zabbits, Karen, Bash; the office volunteers, Kearns, Farber, Johnston; Duffy from the Wall Street Journal; and the two from Greenpeace, Dunston-Withers and DeLeon. She added "someone else" to the bottom of the list.

She said, "Okay, let's start with the easy ones."

Dan kept eating. *"Are* there any easy ones?"

"Well, I think we can cross Karen off the list, agreed?"

"How 'bout we just write, 'not likely,' beside her name."

Teri groaned. "I think we could write 'not likely' beside everyone." Despite her best efforts the frustration of flailing about in ignorance was building up within her again. She wrote 'not likely,' then she drew an arrow down the entire list.

Trevor's article discussed the background of each and every person in the house, but nothing ominous was mentioned. None of these people qualified for 'likely.'

A gentle vibration passed through the floor and the walls. From the window she could see the sky begin to move. Palm trees and white buildings coasted by. The ship was rotating, slowly edging away from the wharf. They could see the convention center and the parking garage. They could see the roadblock back in place. Then the causeway came into view and the bascule bridge. Quickly the *Sea Fantasy* was in the cut and gathering steam. The beach passed, then all there was was rippling blue ocean and a darkening mauve sky.

How long would their lucky streak last? How could things be so marvelous and terrible at the same time?

She sat and stared at her list of names. Then, frustrated, Teri got up and turned on the television. She clicked around to find CNN and found it just as the weather ended and the broadcast went to commercial. She turned the sound down.

Dan was looking through the notes, then pushed them away. "We're getting bogged down in the same thought patterns."

He took a fresh sheet of paper. "Let's try something different." He started a time chart. First entry:

Scranton. Hill is a teacher.

Beneath that he wrote:

Meets fellow teacher Karen.

Each sentence was a new line:

> *They marry.*
> *Hill runs for city council.*
> *He wins.*
> *Hill seeks senate nomination.*
> *Wins over Tasker, a huge upset.*
> *Hill elected to senate.*
> *In senate, Hill begins to make a name for himself.*
> *He stands up against numerous special interest groups.*

Dan jotted down nine different groups and Teri added three more. Next he added:

> *Hill runs for President.*
> *Leading in the primaries.*
> *Hill is murdered.*

Teri stopped him. "Just a second, we know more about the events just before the murder. They're important."

Dan struck off:

> *Hill is murdered.*

Together, Dan and Teri agreed on:

> *Tasker meets with Hill.*
> *Tasker accuses Hill of foul play in winning Senate nomination.*
> *At 8:05 Hill calls CNN to arrange an important press conference for the next day.*
> *Someone comes to Hill's study.*

Dan put a question mark behind that.

> *They argue.*

Another question mark.

> *Hill is murdered.*

No question mark.

Teri enters Hill's office and witnesses the murderer fleeing.

They contemplated the sequence.

"The coincidence of Tasker visiting the night of the murder—that's what stands out."

"Sure. But don't overlook Bash," Dan added. "We know Hill was alive when Tasker left, it was *after* the Tasker meeting that Hill phoned CNN."

"He could have come back."

Dan nodded. "Yes, I guess so."

"And the press conference, if we only knew why he called it . . ."

They didn't know what Hill planned to announce. They didn't know what Andy Bash was doing there, or if it was unusual. They didn't know if there was someone not on their list, someone who had snuck in from the street, an assassin hired by a special interest group who was clever enough to use a weapon from the scene to kill Hill to confuse investigators. They didn't know how to find the answers either, or even how to work their way closer to the truth.

Suddenly they were both staring at the television.

The picture was a live shot, taken from the sky at dusk. The sea was sparkling, gold specs cavorted on oily black waves.

The announcer appeared. Over his left shoulder the camera caught the cruise ship, an amusement park of lights steaming across the water. *"If we could see in those port windows, in one of the cabins we would find the accused murderer, Teri Peterson, and her companion, star hockey*

player Dan Parent. It is quite likely they can spot our he-
licopter in the sky above their heads at this very moment."

Teri jumped up. She went to the large window and stared
out into the night. She could see the flashing red light of
the helicopter.

Dan went to the cabin door. He put his hand on the
handle. He waited, trying to listen, and hearing nothing he
cautiously started to turn the handle. It wouldn't turn. He
tried harder. Teri could see the muscles flex in his forearm.

As if the announcer read his mind, he said, *"They have*
a guard at the door. Authorities have determined that it is
easier to keep the fugitives locked in their cabin. We are
told their cabin has been sealed until they reach Nassau,
where they will be apprehended. This will not occur for
about eight hours. The ship has changed course and is
skipping the planned stopover at Horizon Key, and is now
heading straight for Nassau at top speed."

Teri continued to stare, transfixed. She was stunned.
Slipping away on another out-of-body experience, the only
thought she could muster was one of amazement: *This can't*
be happening to me. There was the same graduation picture
on the screen, and her name. Now a picture of Dan was
shown beside hers. *Poor Dan.* She had found her knight in
shinning armor and promptly ruined his life. This was happening. This was all real. She just couldn't believe it.

And there was no way *this* could possibly be construed
as good. They were cornered.

Dan didn't smile or make light of things. He paced
around the little cabin, examining the walls, ceilings, the
window, the light fixtures. He looked for air ducts or access
holes. It was a small cabin and he was quickly forced to

give up. They weren't going anywhere. Not until Nassau.

The television flickered and switched to the live shot of the ship and the sea and the night sky taken from the helicopter. *"Of course CNN will maintain live coverage every inch of the way. We will continue to follow the* Sea Fantasy *with frequent updates. In the meantime, we are preparing a discussion group on the situation. As we get that set up, here is a little background on the principle characters in this unfolding drama. We'll start with the murder victim, Thomas Jefferson Hill."*

Dan and Teri exchanged a searching glance.

Dan said, "Don't panic. It's going to be okay."

Teri threw out a question with her eyes: how could *this* be okay?

"Least we know the situation. We still have some time."

"A little time and a lot of pressure."

He nodded.

Before their eyes the announcer was saying, *". . . city councilman in Wilkes-Barre, Pennsylvania. He ran for the Senate where he was considered very much an outsider and a very, very long shot at best."*

Teri asked, "You like pressure?"

Dan shrugged. "Sort of gets the blood percolating."

Teri quipped back at him, "My blood was already percolating quite nicely." She took a deep breath.

". . . the party responded to his message, especially his honesty, and he upset the overwhelming favorite, Ron Tasker."

Teri could only half-listen to the television. "I find it's easier to think without a lot of pressure. But I guess—Stanley Cup playoffs—you're used to it."

"I guess." Dan shrugged. "But, I bet the life of every school teacher holds a lot more stress than any hockey player."

"School teacher," she scoffed. It didn't look like she'd ever find out.

Dan said, "There are always a couple of troublemakers in every class."

"You?" she asked.

"I was an angel." But his smile confirmed her suspicions. She wanted to know everything about him. She wanted to know his favorite color, food, music and movie, and what he was like as a kid.

"Now, if the name Ron Tasker seems familiar to you it's because he's presently running for governor in the state of Pennsylvania."

Dan watched. He shook his head. "Seems to keep coming back to Tasker."

Teri repeated the obvious. "He *was* there in the pit that night."

"Yes."

"Coincidence?"

Dan didn't shrug.

How could they know? How could they find out? Somehow they had to find out. Teri wasn't going to give up. She was going to run the facts through her mind over and over again. She didn't care how frustrating it was. She would sort it out.

Hill won a critical nomination vote over Tasker. He benefited from a spurious scandal story. Tasker confronts Hill; Hill is murdered; so Tasker had a motive. Yet it didn't seem right. She watched Tasker on television. He didn't *seem* to be a murderer. He wasn't a crushed and bitter man, he was running for public office anew.

"It wasn't Tasker," she said finally. "Two reasons: one, why would he wait for years?"

"Maybe he just found out."

Teri frowned. Nothing was simple. "Okay, so if he figures Hill victimized him and came to kill the guy, why just hope to grab a weapon at the scene?"

"Good point. But maybe he didn't plan to kill him at all, just accuse him, and somehow things got nasty. Hill denied it or something."

"But it wasn't like Tasker became a bitter man obsessed with revenge—he went on to become a congressman and was running for governor. I saw some article speculating that he might even run for President in four years."

Dan said, "I agree Tasker is not likely. But are there any likely's? We need a likely."

Teri's mind raced. *What about all the special interest groups, any of them could have . . . but why use such a clumsy method, a kitchen knife? An assassin wouldn't use a steak knife. That pointed to sudden anger. What about Karen?* Teri knew she disliked the fishbowl her husband's career had made of their lives. She couldn't believe that either; you love someone, you support their dreams. *Bash was there that night, did they argue about something? Bash worked for Mercer, he was his right-hand-man. Maybe Mercer wanted to be President and decided it was Hill that stood in his way. People have killed for a lot less.* Her head was spinning, and she was desperate to leap to any conclusion at all.

The television picture changed to footage of the last Stanley Cup playoffs. They were discussing Dan. The goalie barely moved, shifting just enough to block the puck, then thwarting a series of shots, like an invincible human wall.

Teri flopped forward on the bed and watched. She watched, save after save, until the series ended, then she mumbled, "Wow. That's not luck."

Dan wasn't watching. He tapped the pen on the pad.

She was no further ahead than she had been the moment she climbed up onto Dan's boat. She couldn't think of anyone who had a strong enough reason to kill Mr. Hill. She thought of all the senseless murders that took place in the world. *Did murderers even have to have a good reason?*

She went back to the beginning and tried to put it together again. She started with the teaching jobs, the city counsel, the nomination, the senate record.

She was getting angry with her own inability to sort it out. "I'm not getting anywhere."

Dan nodded.

"Is the answer here and we're missing it?"

"I don't know." He came and stretched out on the bed beside her.

Teri snuggled into his arms. "I've got to relax. I can't concentrate. I've got to try and relax."

He turned off the sound of the television. It was hard to forget the helicopter and the television cameras, but somehow those thoughts had to be pushed aside.

They lay huddled together on the bed, and for some reason she started telling him about her imaginary scrapbook and how she would like to fill up a few more pages.

She felt washed out and hung up to dry, and swayed a little in the imaginary sun and faint breeze.

Chapter Eleven

"Tell me about your childhood."

"My childhood?" When he spoke she felt the motion of his chin rubbing against her cheek.

"Yes. Tell me anything."

Dan considered that and she began to worry that he'd decline. Surely they had more important things to discuss, but would they ever be able to talk like this again?

"Your mother?"

"I have no recollection of my mother. I understand she left when I was very young."

"I'm sorry. Your dad signed you up for hockey?"

"Yes, I was a latecomer. All the other kids had started when they were three or four."

"Three!"

"You should see a bunch of three year olds playing

hockey." She could feel the muscles flex as Dan smiled at the memory. "Dressed in tiny equipment."

"Can they skate?"

"Yes. No, not really, but they sure have fun. They lean on their sticks and shuffle their feet as fast as they can—which is incredibly fast, their skates are just a blur—but they barely move at all. When they get up to the puck they flail their stick, which was the only thing holding them upright. Whether they hit the puck or not, they fall to the ice face first, feet still racing a mile a minute." Dan chuckled again.

Teri smiled. For a moment she forgot the hopelessness of her plight, their plight.

"Since I was the new guy and I skated like a three-year-old, I got stuck in goal."

"But you were good there."

"Sure. I was too slow, couldn't get out of the way fast enough, so the pucks kept hitting me. They were fooled into thinking I was pretty good."

"A career is born. Tell me more."

Reluctantly, Dan continued. "Unlike other kids I never had the burning desire to make it to the NHL. But I guess I was dumb enough and slow enough to be a good goalie, so pretty soon I was missing half my school days to travel to hockey tournaments. When I was fifteen I moved away from home to play, then at sixteen I quit school, because I was rarely there anyway. Pretty soon it was hockey or nothing for me. Man, I was as dumb as a bag full of pucks. My dad was excited and very proud. I wanted to turn pro just so I could buy him a new car—I remember thinking that.

So that's what happened. I was drafted when I was eigh-
teen. Moved to Chicago. Sat on the bench. Played in one
game. Oh, and I became a bit of a party animal. Then I
was traded a few times, moved to Las Vegas, Norfolk, Her-
shey, Quebec City, Syracuse and Newfoundland. Then the
Toronto Maple Leafs called. They were desperate. A rash
of injuries had wiped them out of goalies. They wanted me
to sit on their bench as a backup for a couple of games, so
I did. Then, in the second game I was there, the starter was
getting shellacked. The coach was going ballistic. He was
fed up with all his players. The team had quit playing. They
were losing, seven to one, in the second period, so the
coach yanked the goalie, sat down all his regulars and sent
in the subs. I let the first shot in. A soft one right between
the pads. I was so scared I didn't even move—which is
sort of my trademark." He laughed harder this time.

"Then?"

"We lost, eight-three, but I was lucky. I got over my
jitters, made some saves, then found out I'm starting the
next game. You know the rest, I played like I'd never
played before. The pucks just kept hitting me, every little
move stopped a puck. It was crazy."

"Your dad must have been very proud."

"Well . . ." Dan's throat became constricted. "Yes. He
saw the first couple of games of the playoffs. Then he got
sick. I knew he was sick but—fifth game of the finals, he
was *very* sick. I couldn't talk to him. I convinced myself
he wanted me to play. I mean, if we won the game, the
series, the season would be over. After the game I was
going to bring the Stanley Cup right into his hospital room

and put it on the bed beside him and he could sleep with it."

"You didn't go to him, you played."

"Yes. They say he died about the same time I ripped up my knee."

"And you feel guilty?"

"Sure I do."

"And that's why you quit hockey?"

"Maybe."

"Maybe?"

"Maybe."

Mentally, Teri slipped away for a moment to think. She didn't want to pry anymore but time was running out. These were the last precious moments they could spend together. "Tell me more."

"There is no more."

"So, why'd you quit?"

"I just don't want to play hockey."

"You loved your father. You feel guilty."

Now, she thought, *this isn't ending on a pleasant note, is it? Do I want laughs, giggles? No, this is good. This is real.* "Dan, I think I've got this figured out." She spoke slowly. "You haven't gotten over your father's death, you feel guilty. Hockey makes you remember and feel bad. But I don't believe you never loved the game, you couldn't have worked to become a star if you hadn't loved to play. I heard the way you reminisced about the three-year-olds."

"Is it that simple?"

"No." She swallowed. "I'm sorry, it's not simple at all. I'm sorry."

"Nothing is simple, is it?"

*   *   *

"We've got about an hour." Dan went over to the port-hole. He could only see the ship's lights sparkling against the black waves. Teri pressed against his back. The helicopter and its red flasher whooshed along the side of the ship. They stood there until they could see the lights appear from Paradise Island.

As she was thinking about how much she wanted to talk about and how little time they had, he said, "Collecting more pages for your scrapbook?"

She smiled. "Always hoping to."

"I think I've already filled up my scrapbook."

"They're imaginary. You can have as many as you want."

"Well you didn't tell me that. That's good. That's very good."

He kissed her.

The ship altered course and new shore lights swung into view.

"We should get ready."

Teri gasped. "I still can't believe any of this. I didn't kill anyone. I should never have run. I don't know why I ran away."

"They were shooting at you."

"Yes, but I should never have involved you. I'm sorry. This is all so incredible. I still can't believe any of this is happening."

With his hand on her chin he drew her eyes up to his. "I love you," he said.

"That's the only part I want to believe."

"Good. That's the only part that's going to last."

It was wonderful to be in his arms. She tried not to think that these last precious moments would have to satisfy her for a long time, for a lifetime. Beyond the window the helicopter flailed by. Beyond the window the lights grew.

She pushed aside her anger. *The moment,* she thought, *the moment. The moment was bliss.* She had lived her entire life without such moments as Dan provided. She felt blessed, this moment, that these moments would carry her through, would comfort her and warm her forever. They would have to. She was going to jail.

"I'm going to check how much time we have." Dan turned up the television. "See if anything has changed. Maybe someone has confessed."

They were rolling a clip of Karen Hill. She looked drawn and pale. "He was withdrawing from the race. That's what the press conference was called for, to announce his withdrawal. I was selfish, I didn't want to share him, but I think it was because of me. He was very anxious and agitated. I'd never seen him so angry.'

"I brought him up his supper, and he told me he had to withdraw. He was on the phone asking to set up a press conference for the next day. He was very upset. I wanted to stay with him, but he said he had a few things to take care of first, then we could talk. He was going to withdraw."

Dan found the timeline he had started.

Teri said, "He was withdrawing because of Karen?"

"No." Dan was writing, he looked up. "That's not quite what she said."

"He was withdrawing."

They continued to discuss it as the television cycled through a series of commercials.

"Yes, but she only speculated it was because of her. She never said that he *said* it was because of her. And he did say he had a couple of things to take care of before they could discuss it. He didn't specifically say it was because of her."

"But that's the feeling she got. She was there, she knew him."

"He was angry. She said he was angrier than she had ever seen him. Why would he be angry if he was withdrawing for her? What was he angry about? She never pressured him, that's what you said. She supported his dream. But he was angrier than she had ever seen him before—why suddenly angry? There *has* to be a better reason."

Dan added to his time line. Between *Spoke with Tasker* and *8:05 phoned CNN*, he wrote, *Told wife he was withdrawing*. Teri watched over his shoulder.

On the pad Dan inserted another line. *He had a couple of things to do*. The next line was, *Hill murdered*.

In the background the television announcer said, *"Warren Zabbits was not even aware of the press conference. He thought it must have been of a highly personal nature. Mr. Zabbits was Hill's longest serving and closest advisor. If Hill was going to quit, Zabbits would know."*

The woman beside the announcer responded, *"I think that just confirms the announcement was of a personal nature, a withdrawal for family considerations."*

"So how does Ms. Peterson become involved?"

The ship was near the harbor. The shore was close beside the ship. Dan and Teri could see a small lighthouse. They saw tall whitecaps curl in from the ocean and smash upon the rocks and the foam burst up into the sky.

CNN broke away from the panel and switched to a reporter on the wharf. *"It's a warm night here in Nassau, very pleasant, though the Nassau weather office is forecasting a heavy thundershower. The threat of rain hasn't discouraged a crowd from gathering."* The camera panned away from the reporter and scanned the crowd.

Dan watched the television screen. Seeing Trevor he started to point him out to Teri when suddenly he saw Clay Hedoby. "What's he doing here?"

"Trevor?" Teri had recognized him as well. She was actually feeling glad to see him.

"No, Hedoby."

"Hedoby? How did he get here?"

"It's just a quick flight from Florida. CNN has told the world exactly where we are. Anybody could be here." There were hundreds of people, townspeople, police, media, people from other cruise ships.

The reporter continued, *"We can't see the cruise ship yet, Paul, though I'm told they see it plainly from Fort Montague up on the hill behind me. Just a second, there it is. I can see the lights now as it enters the harbor."*

The camera showed the bow of the great ship slowly approaching. He quickly described the scene.

The studio anchorman was back on, superimposed over the moving picture of the *Sea Fantasy*. *"The way they plan to do this is quite simple. At present, as I'm sure you are all aware, Parent and Peterson are locked in their cabin, with guards posted at the door. All passengers aboard the* Sea Fantasy *have been asked to remain in their respective*

*cabins. After the ship docks, members of the Royal Baham-
ian Constabulary and a unit from American Special Weapons and Tactics will board the ship and remove the
accused, taking them immediately to the airport for a flight
back to the United States."*

The picture flipped back to the dock. Ms. Grant stood
beside the reporter. He introduced her. In the top right corner of the screen a picture of the brightly lit cruise ship
remained. A pulse of sheet lightning rolled across the heav-
ens.

Anne Grant glanced up to the sky then waited through
the rumble of thunder before saying: *"I'm still worried
someone will try to kill Ms. Peterson. There has been a
number of attempts on her life in the past few days."*

Teri, tired, turned down the television. "There is too
much to think about. I'm getting confused. The only important thing is who killed Hill."

"Start at the beginning."

No, not the beginning, she thought with a barely suppressed groan.

"Somebody killed Mr. Hill," he spoke calmly. "It wasn't
an accident. Therefore, they had a reason."

"Right," Teri agreed. "It was most likely someone in the
compound, and they did it on the spur of the moment because they did it in a particularly violent and impromptu
way." She had an inspiration. "So they came into Hill's
study not intending to kill him, something else brought
them into the house, and whatever provoked them occurred
after they were in the study."

"Something Hill said?"

"Yes?" It was a question. She wasn't sure. She had to

think. *Wouldn't it have to be something Hill had said?* "Someone killed him just because he said he was withdrawing?" That didn't sound reasonable.

He shook his head. "No, there has to be something more than that. You might get angry that the person you'd worked hard for was quitting, but you don't kill them."

"Why was he withdrawing?"

"That's got to be the key." Dan looked back to his sheet. "Hill spoke to Tasker. He was angry when he told Karen he was withdrawing. He phoned CNN to arrange the press conference, but he planned to do at least one more thing before he turned in for the night."

Dan and Teri stalled again. Everything Teri could think of had been said before. No new ideas came to mind. It wasn't going to happen. They weren't going to figure it out.

Finally Dan muttered, "What were the things he wanted to do?"

"I don't know!"

Dan remained calm. "What kind of things would he logically want to do? He had suddenly decided to withdraw. He had told his wife. He had arranged a press conference. What else would he do?"

The vibration in the floor ceased. A red tug came alongside their window. They could see the man at the helm. A moment later they could feel the tug nudging the bow of the ship in towards the dock.

In an attempt to keep the wheels turning, Teri responded by asking, "Tasker told Hill something, something that prompted him to withdraw. He must have. We know Hill beat Tasker in a huge upset for the Senate nomination.

There was some kind of foul play in the win." Then she argued with herself, "But I can't believe Hill would use underhanded tactics."

On the television they watched the fat dock lines being set. The brisk wind whipped a crew man's hair.

"Did Tasker threaten to blow the whistle on Hill? But nobody killed Tasker, it was Hill that was murdered."

The ramp was extended from the side of the ship. The dock crew stood back. The police came aboard, dozens of them.

"And Tasker didn't kill Hill, because Karen spoke to her husband after Tasker. Somebody else must have come to see him after that. Who?"

"We don't know who, but we have it narrowed down to just a few people."

"Do we know why they came? We know they didn't come to kill him because, they didn't bring a weapon, right? They came for some other reason."

"Then they had words with Hill."

"Anger, murder."

"Hill was angry, we know that, but he didn't murder anyone."

Teri was frustrated. The wheels were spinning.

Hand-in-hand they waited to be arrested.

Her mind leapt from thought to idea. If Hill hadn't been murdered she would never have met Dan. Surely she couldn't be glad he was murdered. That just proved how confused she was becoming.

"What's taking so long?" Teri asked.

"I'm not in a hurry. Are you in hurry?"

She wrestled with an urge to laugh. "No, I guess not."

"I hope they get lost. It's a big ship." Dan said, "Let's reconstruct the crime. One more time."

"I can't. I can't think. No more. Let's just enjoy the last precious moments." She squeezed his hand.

The television had shown nothing but the outside of the cruise ship. The announcers had run out of things to say and they kept repeating themselves, waiting.

Dan and Teri could hear people beyond the cabin door.

"Are you okay?"

She nodded. Amazing, she felt okay. "You?"

Dan grinned, weakly. "I think I'm at peace about this."

"Some things just can't be taken away. Stone walls do not a prison make, nor iron bars a cage. I feel free. Thanks to you, I will always feel free."

Dan nodded.

"Except," Teri said, "I feel bad for you. I'm sorry."

"Don't be. I wouldn't change a thing."

"Nothing?"

"Well, maybe the ending, the part where we don't prove your innocence. It'd be nice to change that bit." Teri snickered.

"When they come, we have to be careful."

"Yes."

"Nothing crazy."

"No."

"Alive we can continue to fight, even if it is from jail."

It was silent again in the hall, then a humming sound began.

Dan stepped forward. "Ready?" He reached for the door lock.

"No."

Dan gripped the lock toggle in his hand but stopped.

"I won't forget the card," she said.

He couldn't help smiling. "Better not."

"It's all over, isn't it? This is the end."

"No, It's not the end." He removed his hand from the lock. Instead he looked at her. He could see she was suffering, valiantly trying to remain brave, but suffering. "I've got one idea left."

"Really?"

He was nodding when the door popped open. The team rushed in. Men shouted at Teri. She wasn't sure what they were saying but she understood the gist of it. She only moved to bring her hands up into the air, palms forward.

They were quickly surrounded. The cabin was full. The hall was crowded by men in dark bulletproof vests, big boots and helmets with little microphones and sinister-looking weapons. The men looked identical, kept barking out orders, and she still had no idea what they were saying. Her hands came down. She was cuffed behind her back.

"Dan, what idea?" She hissed. "Have you figured it out?"

Dan turned to look at her, but he didn't answer. He didn't smile or grin. He mouthed, "I love you."

She couldn't answer. Fear had gripped her heart, it missed three beats, then began to pound. There were no tricks left.

Someone was reading her her rights, she heard that.

What idea, she wondered. *Did he know?* She ran through the possibilities in her mind. A small army of men were forming up around her. She had a man on each side of her, clutching her arm just above the elbow. They continued to yell at her.

She had a sudden thought. No one would have just wandered up to Hill's upstairs office at that time of night, so it was either because something terribly important had happened, or because Hill had summoned them. He told Karen he'd be along in a minute, first he wanted to do a couple of things. *What things?* He was angry, said he was withdrawing, but there was one more thing he wanted to do . . . what? Was there someone else he wanted to talk to? She considered that as the men marched her into the corridor behind Dan.

Wouldn't he want to speak to his staff? The people who had worked so hard, some of them unpaid volunteers, on his behalf. He'd want to tell them he was withdrawing, that's the kind of man he was, but he didn't do that. He didn't tell them, no one knew. Only Karen knew.

The corridor was choked with men from various law enforcement agencies. They formed up around her and moved forward. They began to pass white-coated stewards. Some doors were open a crack—people were peeking out at the spectacle. From inside the cabins she could hear televisions; she could hear announcers discussing the weather. The *weather?*

The entourage came to the top of the stairs and the great hall.

She tried to think. *Who? Wouldn't he want to speak to the men and women who had worked for him? Yes.*

Halfway down the wide staircase, she could see the purser's reception desk. The dining room was empty except for a couple of waiters in red jackets. Stewards were posted everywhere. Other stewards trailed along behind the entourage.

But Hill didn't explain the situation to his team.

Teri saw the portal where she had entered a few hours earlier. It was open. A cool breeze swept in. She could smell the sea and rain. She was on the top of the ramp. There was an ear-shattering crack of thunder and lightning lit up the night sky. Teri could see the gathered crowd as the police led her down.

Mr. Hill hadn't told his team about the withdrawal. If he had, surely someone would have said so. Tasker told Hill something that enraged him. Probably something about the upset win in Pennsylvania. Teri still had trouble believing Hill was capable of any sort of treachery, but the evidence was there. Hill told his wife he was withdrawing, he phoned CNN to arrange a press conference. It had something to do with the upset win over Tasker. So it must be because of that scandal.

Teri neared the bottom of the ramp. The group stopped. The wind suddenly began to swirl and tear at her.

Dan glanced back. The man beside him jerked his arms to twist him forward.

A wall of rain swept across the wharf. Suddenly it was chaos. People began to run in all directions. One of the men at the front of the pack spoke into the little microphone on his helmet. The rain hit, and everything was submerged in the torrent. She could see nothing but rain, hear nothing but shouts muffled by the thrumming downpour. The men beside her clenched her arms and pulled her down to her knees. They had lost control of the situation.

The rain pummeled. The wind whipped the rain at them like pellets. The police hovered close around her.

Teri closed her eyes. She saw Mr. Hill again. Surely he'd

call Zabbits, but Warren Zabbits said he didn't know anything about the press conference. Zabbits had been with Hill since his first senate campaign. Surely he'd tell Zabbits.

She imagined the conversation.

Hill in an angry voice: "Warren, I'm pulling out of the presidential race."

Zabbits: "Why?"

Hill: "Tasker is going to reveal what I did to him in the Pennsylvania senate nomination."

Teri thought that that sounded possible, but not quite right. She still couldn't envision Hill stooping to such underhanded tactics. She tried it again.

Hill in an angry voice: "Tasker is going to reveal what we did to him."

How about: "Tasker told me what *you* did to him in the Pennsylvania senate nomination."

Teri played with the words once more. She listened in her mind. Hill: "Tasker proved to me that *you* sabotaged his bid for the Pennsylvania senate nomination. We won unfairly, therefore I will have to withdraw, and tomorrow I will apologize to the American people."

Perhaps they argued. Hill's reputation would be tarnished, but Zabbits would be ruined. Incensed, he may have grabbed the first weapon at hand, the knife.

Teri whispered with wonder in her voice, "Zabbits?"

In her memory of that terrible night, the man fleeing even looked like Zabbits. It all fit.

The rain stopped as suddenly as it came. The front passed. The gusty, swirling winds died down and now blew brisk and steady from the north. She was drenched. The men hauled her to her feet. She was pushed forward.

The rain had caught everyone. People had sought whatever shelter they could find.

"Zabbits," she whispered. She felt certain it was right. There was no proof, but it fit together. And Zabbits was the one with the gun that had tried to kill her. She remembered the wild look in his eyes, he was trembling, and she thought he was afraid of *her!*

"Zabbits," she said loudly.

The men at her side shook her.

It was Zabbits, she felt sure of it. Maybe there was hope . . . somehow.

Epilogue

Trevor wore a gray suit and a fedora with a teal ribbon. She smiled as he sat down beside her.

"Well?" He nodded to center ice. "You like it?"

Teri nodded. "Incredible."

"Can I quote you on that?"

She laughed gently.

The raucous crowd dispersed, though a few remained, milling about in one cluster at the bottom of the long concrete stairs.

Trevor said, "Splendid that he confessed, eh?"

Teri nodded. She didn't say it but thought to herself *He had to, really.* Her fingerprints were all over the knife, but there was a little corner of a thumb print that matched only Warren Zabbits. Once the police established that, it was impossible for him to deny.

"Difficult to comprehend what Zabbits was thinking."

Teri had already put that all behind her. Anne Grant explained it best when she said, "He just lost it. He couldn't understand what Hill's problem was. He could be President, but instead he was going to throw it all away. Zabbits was incensed. He grabbed the knife and killed him, but then he panicked. When he shot at you, he was probably half-crazy, probably never even considered the possibility that you had never recognized him. Then he hired people to kill you."

"Well," Trevor said as he stood, "I've got to run and file my story."

Dan was the first one out of the team dressing room. He immediately looked up and saw her sitting alone in the stands, but he couldn't come to her—first he had to sign every program, card and sweater presented to him.

Teri waited for him to finish then said, "I feel like a hockey groupie."

"Told you not to come."

"You kidding? I wouldn't have missed this for the world."

"Like your first game?"

"I loved it."

Dan looked down at his feet. A slight grin worried the corners of his mouth. "Would you like to go out for dinner?"

"Sure."

He took her hand, and they left together.